Seasons On the Dark Side

Diane Arrelle

JERSEY PINES INK

JERSEY PINES INK

This is a work of fiction. Names, characters, businesses, places, events, locales and incidents are either the products of the author's imagination or used in a fictitious manner. Any resemblance to actual persons, living or dead, or actual events is purely coincidental.

Copyright © 2018 Jersey Pines Ink, LLC

For information, address the publisher at:
JerseyPinesInk.com

Cover art— Dar Albert, Wicked Smart Designs

ISBN: 978-1-948899-017

DEDICATION

This book is dedicated to

my mother-in-law,

Eileen Leacock,

my sister-in-law Sheila Leacock,

and to the memory of my

father-in-law, John M. Leacock

and brother-in-law, Robert Leacock.

CONTENTS

WINTER

SPRING

SUMMER

AUTUMN

WINTER

WALKIES

"Come on, Hankie, take Poochikins for his walkies."

Hank wondered why he was even with Sherry. She was the girl-friend from hell as far as he could tell. Whiny, bitchy, moody, lazy, and spoiled rotten. She was always making Hank jump through hoops just to get a little cold ass.

And sadly, he leapt every time she asked because he'd never been with such a beautiful woman before. Sexy trumped pride every time.

Grimacing at Sherry's new pound hound, Hank got up and put on his winter coat. "Awfully cold out tonight," he muttered at the bristly mutt who was staring back at him with total doggie disdain. Hank grunted, grabbed the leash and attached it to the rhinestone collar of the toy sized dog. "Let's go Poochikins. Time for a walk. Gonna get you out of here and man you up. No one, not even a dog, deserves all this bling and humiliation."

He tugged the little canine out the door, down the elevator, and out of the apartment building into the cold winter's night. "Well Pooch, I can call you Pooch when we're alone right? Well, Pooch, I don't know why she went to the shelter and got you yesterday. I mean, we were barely happy without having a pet to make life more complicated."

Poochikins snarled at the few people rushing by on the sidewalk. "Thank God we live in this high rise, huh Pooch, away from the cars and crowds," Hank said. "Now do your doggie thing so we can get back inside where it's warm."

To Hank's amazement, Poochikins surged ahead, almost yanking his arm off. "Shit, that little mutt is strong," he muttered and ran to keep up. Suddenly the dog, which in the streetlight seemed larger and even more bristlier, stopped and began digging in someone's postage stamp sized front yard. Hank pulled the leash but the dog didn't budge. Giving up the fight, he looked around and saw no one watching the mutt tear up the lawn. "Ok, have a canine ball, it ain't my yard, huh pup?"

Hank stood leash in hand waiting as the dog disappeared and the dirt flew out of the hole.

Just as he decided that enough was enough, a creature that could pass for Poochikin's giant twin bounded from the hole. Growling at Hank, it howled like hell then turned and jumped back down, yanking Hank with him before he could drop the leash.

The hole, a seemingly bottomless pit, ended abruptly and Hank found himself face to face with a demon. Poochikins, now a monstrous image of a dog, growled as the demon smiled and said, "Thanks for returning my hellhound. Been waiting for him to bring me some help."

Hank stared at the demon and demon dog and felt nauseous. He had a really, really bad feeling about being dragged to the Underworld. "Uh, yeah, sure, glad to be of service. Now if you'd just show me the way back, I already have a job--"

"Gee pal, I'd love to repay you for returning my dog, but we just don't do that sort of thing down here. Good turns are really frowned upon."

Hank felt sweat on his face and torso. It ran down his back in rivulets. "But … but … "

The demon frowned and patted the hellhound.

What a god-awful sight, Hank decided as his stomach lurched.

"The dog says you were nice to it, changed his dumb human name and all, so tell you what, you stay here and be my new assistant forever and I'll try to make it easier. Sound good? You get used to the heat after a few decades and the perks can be nice."

Hank shuddered, making an involuntary whimpering noise.

The demon's frown deepened. "Or . . . I could send you back up as a miniature hellhound and you can bring me a replacement assistant. I really gotta get help, the workload is hell."

The demon licked his lips and smiled, which Hank decided was even more disturbing than his frown. "You know, your girlfriend's really hot, she'd work out quite well."

Hank thought for about two seconds and howled his consent. After all, she'd picked out the damned dog in the first place and he always thought of her as the girlfriend from Hell, so why not. The way he saw it, she'd fit in perfectly fine down here and he'd revert back to a man, free and topside once again.

He just hoped that poor kinda-nice demon and his faithful hellhound wouldn't suffer too much.

A SKY FULL OF
SHOOTING STARFISH

My name is Suzie.

You are living in my house, sleeping in my bed.

And someday, hopefully you will go through those boxes in the attic and save me.

I know the place is a rental and I know you are the fourth person to take up residence here since my disappearance. I bet you don't even know about me, about the woman who disappeared one night without a trace. Sure, they suspected foul play or maybe suicide, but that's not the case at all. Nope, not at all. It doesn't matter. All you have to do is go through those boxes in the attic.

I tried to tell my story to the others before you, but it didn't work. They slept too soundly, didn't have enterable dreams. I hope you are different. I hope you hear me.

I've lived all my life in Arkansas. Never saw the ocean, never saw an iceberg, never saw anything but Arkansas. Not a bad place to live, but I'm a Pisces, I needed to be near the sea.

I went to the mall one day and threw a wishing penny or ten into the fountain, then I turned and saw the calendar store. I was drawn to it like a fish to a worm on a hook, suckered in by the calendar in the window: Seascapes To Live By. I was shopping for Christmas presents for my friends and the only family I have, my stepsister, and I thought, *wow, a calendar what a great gift idea.*

I couldn't believe the prices, shocking! But I didn't care because I was charging it all and I wasn't worried about the bill. I figured I'd pay it off when I could, a little bit at a time. I wonder if my debt has been forgiven or forgotten after three years of being one of the missing? Oh well, I'm drifting off course.

I looked at all the selections, there were hundreds of varieties, styles, and sizes, but I couldn't take my eyes off that one with the pictures of the ocean. I thumbed through it, enjoying the views of turquoise blue Caribbean water lapping softly against pristine white sand, angry gray waves smashing against rugged New England cliffs, glaciers calving, creating icebergs, and California sunsets with surfers silhouetted against the red sky. There were even pictures taken underwater of colorful fish swimming in the reefs and my favorite, the moon shinning down on an endless expanse of black water covered with shimmering dots of silvery reflection.

I know it was dumb but I bought every copy of the seascapes there and then took them home and gift wrapped them all. I bet they are still up there in one of the boxes, gifts long forgotten, memories belonging to a lost soul.

When I finished wrapping them I had one left over. Well not really, but I decided that my secret Santa at work, the crab working three desks over from me, didn't deserve such a nice gift. So I kept it for myself.

Christmas was still two weeks away so I put them all under the tree except the one I kept for myself. That one I presented to myself with a bottle of Merlot and a lot of PMS. I took a sip of wine and looked at the first picture, the Caribbean beach. Oh, how I longed to feel the warm water as I imagined myself wading slowly out in it. What I secretly knew in my heart was that just out of the frame was the man of my dreams, waving me into the water to join him. I sipped my wine and stroked the image and suddenly the water beneath my fingertips was wet with my tears. I didn't bother to wipe my eyes. I only wiped the picture so it wouldn't be ruined.

I took another drink and turned to February. The glacier! White at the edges and so blue inside as if it had formed around hidden gems. I looked at the giant piece breaking off the main body, caught in the act of calving forever and I tried to hear the rumbling crack like thunder. Again I began to cry because try as I might, I couldn't use any of my other senses, only sight.

I looked at March and saw the storm tossed waves and wondered what it sounded like. I squinted and noticed the ice on the cliff top hanging over the side like daggers. Icicles, them I was familiar with, because although Arkansas is temperate, we had our fair share of icy storms. Pretty enough to look at through a cozy window, but they were not the ocean.

I spent the next few nights drinking wine and taking in the other months. It took so long because I was mesmerized by each scene and the world it represented. Worlds I knew I'd never know, never get to see in real life. I wondered what salty brine tasted like, yeah, I know salty, but it had to be different than plain water and salt. What did each place smell like and how did it sound, the waves of the California coast, the soft, soft lapping water of the Caribbean. It was like watching a horrible accident. I wanted to turn away but couldn't. Well, that was me and my calendar. It was killing me, it made me so sad, and yet I hungered to see more.

It was on the fifth night that it happened. It was the last night of the Geminids, the best meteor shower of the year, at least they were to me. I bundled up and sat outside on a lawn chair looking up to watch the falling stars. I read once that if they fell to Earth and hit the ocean they turned into real starfish, glowing with the inner knowledge that they traveled the universe to end up here under the water forever. A home for them at last. They'd traveled a route I could not, and they were rewarded for their journey's end. I was stuck watching them fall down toward earth as puffs of my frozen breath reached toward the sky.

I was holding my calendar, I never let it go, I needed to feel it, because it meant that much to me. I felt it was magical, just like I secretly still believed in the magic of my lucky four leaf clover, or wishing on my birthday candles, or even wishing on a falling star. Well, that night I had hundreds of falling stars to wish on and I hugged my ocean scenes and wished over and over again: "Take me away from here, let me see all these places myself. Let me live them."

Now that I think back, I should have chosen better wording. Anyway, the best I can figure out, and this is only a guess, mind you, I wished on the one meteorite that made it to the ocean and became that magical starfish. Stupid, I know, but how else could this have happened to me?

One minute, I was sitting in the cold Arkansas night, the next I was in that California sunset sinking like a stone. I struggled, choking as water poured down my throat and through all the shock and fear I couldn't help but think, so this is what the sea tastes like.

I finally remembered how to swim. I rose to the surface and kept my head above water, at least between the rolling, crashing waves. I tumbled head over heels but somehow I always came up for air. I was confused, terrified, and yet so happy because I finally got one of my wishes to come true. I don't know how long I dog paddled through the surf, but suddenly one of those surfing silhouettes became very real and smashed into me, bounced over me, and the world went black.

When I became aware, I was aware of being cold, colder than I've ever been in my life, with chattering teeth and numbing pain shooting daggers of ice through my arms and legs. I wondered, *am I dead? Is this what death feels like?*

But, of course, I was wrong. I wasn't dead at all, I was not that lucky. I was in the icy arctic waters near the glacier. "I want to go home!" I shouted to the sky, but the frozen orb of the sun ignored me. I bobbed, wondering how long I could last, then the iceberg broke. What a sound: magnificent, thrilling, unbelievable. I forgot my misery for just a moment, but the cold was relentless. I thought about the movie Titanic and wondered how anyone could have survived the icy waters. My vision began to close in on itself, and as it narrowed to nothingness, I wondered if I was going to die this time.

Eventually, I became aware of warmth and the call of seagulls. I was waist deep in the warmest, bluest water I've ever experienced. It was perfection. I heard someone calling my name. "Suzie! Suzie, come on and join me already!"

The man of my dreams! He was out so deep he was just a blur on a sailboat. I waded out deeper, but I couldn't get to him. "I'm coming!" I called, and dove under.

No matter how hard I swam he always remained a blur, just out of reach. I kept going until I was so exhausted I rolled onto my back and floated, amazed at the buoyancy of the water. Eventually I closed my eyes, the heat of the sun making me drowsy and I dozed off. Only to wake ...

Never mind, I could go on like this forever. Let me just say, I've spent days under the water with those gaily colored fish and I've learned barracudas are territorial, nasty creatures with razor-like teeth and I learned that reefs are very, very sharp and jagged. I've discovered being thrown against huge rocks at the bottom of those icy cliffs in a violent, bone-chilling sea is a horrible, bone-shattering experience.

I've visited all twelve scenes over and over. I hate to sound ungrateful because how many people really do get to have their wish come true, but I can't take it anymore. California has lots of sharks, and sea lions are not the cute, friendly animals we think they are. The black night sea covered in sparkles gets old quickly, and I've discovered wishing on the moon isn't like wishing on shooting stars. The Caribbean is the most comfortable, but I'm sick of that jerk calling to me all the time then sailing out of reach. I've been wet for what feels like forever and I long for a fluffy towel and a hot latte.

I want to go home, back to Arkansas. I will always love the ocean, always, but if I ever get out of this, I swear I'll be happy looking at pictures and watching it on TV. I've really learned my lesson. Wishes aren't what you expect at all, I suspect they may actually be two-sided, good and bad. Yes, no more wishes for me if I ever get out of this. I swear it.

Now listen, I'll be telling you this story every time you doze off, because it only takes once to hear me. I see you twitching in your sleep. Either you can understand me or it was that right-before-bedtime pizza. I know it's a long shot, but hopefully, you will respond to my call.

Go to the attic and find me, I know the calendar is in one of the boxes. Look for the unwrapped, tear-stained one that is about three years out of date and has the most amazing photographs of the sea. If you peruse it, you'll see me in a picture. I'll just be a speck off in the distance, but you'll see me if you really try. Check all the photos because I tend to move around a lot.

Don't let anything bad happen to that calendar! When we have a scheduled meteor shower, go out and wish on every shooting star. Wish for me to come home again. Wish and wish and wish until it works and if it's not asking too much, perhaps you could also wish that the man of my dreams comes ashore with me. Seriously, what could possibly go wrong with that?

LIGHTING THE WAY

Tess sat at the bar of the luxurious lakefront lodge. She considered ordering a drink, remembered all her meds, then ordered anyway. Sipping her rum and Coke, her first drink in decades, she stared out the huge window and waited. The ice boats whipping across the seemingly endless expanse of Taylorville Memorial Lake held her attention for only a moment. It was strangely quiet; the people all around her weren't talking and laughing like the old days, no, they all sat side by side tapping on machines. She knew they were small computers, phones and games and she sighed. Such a strange world.

"Tess, Tessie is that you?"

She looked up and saw three men standing by her table, two of them well into their senior years, the other in his mid-fifties. She forced a sad smile because she hadn't smiled like she meant it in half a century. "Yes, come sit."

They talked and she ordered another drink. Her head was buzzing and she wasn't sure if it was the alcohol or the fact that she hadn't taken a pill since she got out of the asylum two days ago.

"I'm glad you found me, Mr. Glover," she said. "Somehow I had hoped for more of us."

Mr. Glover nodded his bald head, "There were, but most have died over the last fifty years. All in all, about forty people survived originally, but there were lots of suicides. Oops, sorry."

Tess nodded and ordered another drink. "I was institutionalized, a lovely place that the settlement money paid for all these years. I never tried to kill myself, guess I just wasn't that crazy. I hear voices and suffer from depression instead.

The younger man said, "Look, I was just two when the dam broke but my family is down there. The sun will set soon, why don't we go and pay our respects now."

"Sure, Bobby, good idea. Time to bundle up and go," the third man said. "I haven't been back in two decades. It hurts to remember the town the way it was."

Tess thought about the town, down under the water, buried for all time as well as everyone with it. When the dam burst, she'd been one of the few who somehow survived. She never understood why she lived, or why Jim and the baby had died in their sleep.

But she knew they didn't sleep now, because they called to her all the time. Without her medications, she'd have gone completely mad. Listening to five decades of a baby crying for her mother would drive anyone crazy.

Tess rose, put on her parka, and the four of them went out onto the blue ice that stretched to the horizon that faded into the blinding rays of the setting winter sun.

She shivered and looked back at a foreign landscape. This had once been miles of forest with Taylorville in the center. Now it was a lake and a resort. Probably more people lived around here for work than had lived in the town buried under the water. Funny how life goes on and people benefit from tragedy.

"I'd love to drain this sucker and set things right," Mr. Glover muttered. "Shameful no one ever got buried. Town cemetery's down there, too."

Bobby shrugged. "It's enough that they are memorialized with a plaque," he said, pointing. "The dead are gone."

Tess tilted her head and listened to the sounds she could hear below the wind: the voices calling, the baby crying. She knew differently. "I've heard stories that on nights like this when the sky gets dark and the water is a frozen window, people have seen the town lit up."

"Aw that's crazy!" the third man snapped. "I'm cold, the sun's down, and it's dark. This is just plain dumb. I'm going back for dinner."

They turned to go, but Tess announced, "I'm going to stay a bit." She watched the men retreat and listened to the voices that had been silenced by modern medicine for so many years. She instinctively glanced down, looking for lights or a sign of some kind.

"May I join you?" Bobby asked as he returned. "I'd like to see lights under the ice, too."

They stood side by side in the now black evening and listened to the wind howl through the tall pines surrounding the lake. Suddenly, Tess tensed and dropped to her knees. Desperately clawing at the ice, she screamed, "Look, look, the town is there, see it, see the lights!"

Bobby dropped to his knees as well. "Yes, Tess, I do."

She smiled at him, a real smile, and sighed. "They're down there, you know. Waiting."

Bobby put his arm around Tess's shoulder and said, "This isn't the first time I've been here, Tess. I came about fifteen years ago. I joined them then."

Tess shivered. "A suicide?"

"No, an invitation. And it is extended to you. Shall we?"

Tess didn't hesitate. "Yes."

Without a sound, the ice vanished beneath their feet and she sank down, all cold and all regret gone. Suddenly there was Jim and her baby girl beside her. She gently took her daughter into her arms and smiled. The baby finally stopping crying.

TIPS

The day the world went to hell started out just like any other day. I woke up early to watch infomercials. I love those half-hour long ads and there were now forty-seven channels dedicated to them. I had just finished placing an order for mineral make-up when the infomercial for Never-Dying Grass came on. I watched for a few minutes, wondering why anyone would want a fresh green lawn all year round. Grass is supposed to turn brown and wither in the winter months. I understood why it was such a popular product with the cemetery trade and golf courses, but now the Green Seed Company was trying to target the suburban homeowners. I turned the TV off in disgust and went outside, hugging my robe tighter against the January wind.

And then I stopped short because a dead person was eating my dog.

Actually, having Muffy devoured by a mindless animated corpse wasn't the end of the world for me since the nasty dog had belonged to my late husband, Henry, and I often wished the bitch had joined him. But what I did find disturbing was the fact that it was my late husband, Henry, munching on the mutt.

I stood rooted in the doorway as my deceased spouse rendered Muffy limb from limb and then, while squatting on the ice-rimmed grass, ate each leg. I mean, Henry was never a drumstick kind of guy. No, he had always been the dull steak-and potatoes kind of guy, so much so, in fact, that a coronary had knocked him off his feet forever. I had assumed forever or at least more than five months. God, I'd only gotten his junk out of the house and into the thrift shop last week.

Henry was covered in dirt and starting to decay, I could smell him clear across the yard. I fought off the urge to call to him, after all, I'd seen all the zombie movies and knew what fate awaited anyone who got near them. So I closed and locked, bolted actually, the back door and realized that I never had to refill the dog's water bowl again.

I sat in the kitchen, feeling queasy and wishing the acid jumping up my throat would settle down. I may not have liked the dog, but I hadn't wanted it dead and certainly not shredded and eaten by its master. And the thought I had avoided finally broke through. *Why was Henry a zombie?*

As if in answer, I became aware of pandemonium from outside: screams, cars crashing, gun shots. I decided to switch on the television again. The first 676 stations I turned to consisted of reruns, infomercials, game shows, soaps, talk shows, cooking shows, exercise shows, and evangelists screaming to their god for salvation and to their audience for money. Finally, I found a local news station. All I saw was pretty newscasters describing the scenes around town, and showing videos of zombies in varying states of decay stumbling around with arms outstretched and occasionally eating some stray animals. So far only a few people had been eaten and that was after a group of zombies had walked into a long term care facility for breakfast.

Then the news story switched to the traffic and weather and what movies grossed the highest over the weekend. Obviously zombies may have been the "Big Story" but not big enough to break the station's routine and timetable.

I sat and watched the tube hoping for guidance, but none came. The phone rang and I picked it up to hear my boss, Louie, yelling. Since Louie always yelled, I didn't put much stock into it.

"Rita! Where are you?" he bellowed. "You were due in half an hour ago!"

I thought for a moment and wondered if he was totally mad. "Uh, Louie, didn't you notice that the world seems to be ending? There are zombies outside."

"So?" he yelled. "That means you get a day off? I don't think so. Now get yourself in here by eleven for the lunch crowd."

"Lou, do you really think anyone will be in for lunch?"

"Of course. The special is beef stew or hot roast beef sandwiches, both big sellers!"

I sighed, "I'll try, but if I get eaten by a zombie, you are the first one I'll be coming after."

He laughed. "Rita, if you get eaten by a zombie, you are already on the way to being dumber than they are. They're brain dead for Chrissake. If one comes at you, walk around it."

He made sense so I put on my puffy parka and zipped it tight for extra protection against being eaten, glanced out the front window and went out as soon as the coast was clear. I walked very slowly, constantly on the lookout for anything that moved. I saw a few rotting squirrels trying to figure out how to climb trees but that was about it. I passed the park with grass so green and even, it looked like Astroturf. I shook my head, here it was the dead of winter, the last snowstorm just melted away in last week's rains, and that new Never-Dying Grass grew like it was summer year round.

Lou was right, zombies couldn't really think and since they were in various stages of rot, they couldn't move all that fast either. About seven blocks from my row house, I saw a pair of them, a man dragging his leg and stumbling and a woman right behind him with her dress almost shredded and the flesh on her torso pretty much eaten away. They groaned incoherently, lifted their arms like sleepwalkers, and started for me. My stomach clenched like I was going to throw-up and I swear I felt my blood drop several degrees and turn colder than the wind. I froze, I couldn't think, I couldn't breathe. They were going to get me.

Then just as suddenly as I froze up with fear, the adrenaline kicked in filling me up with internal fire and I turned and crossed the street. I walked briskly away from them and although they tried to follow, I left them to eat my dust. After that, whenever I saw a zombie coming toward me, I just gave it a very wide space and they pretty much just shuffled on like I didn't exist.

I walked the twelve blocks to work and wondered how much thinking they could do with their brains filled with embalming fluids and pretty much the consistency of bread pudding. I mean, they'd been dead a while and I'd read once that fifteen minutes without air pretty much means zero brain function forever.

As I got to the luncheonette, I still wondered what brought on this resurrection of the dear departed. Lou was correct again, much to my utter shock. Customers were filing in and filling all the booths and counter seats. Only it wasn't for the beef, it was the human need to huddle together in the dark. The world was all wrong and people needed to congregate and talk. I hustled for three hours straight serving platters and filling endless coffee cups as the conversations made the time fly.

By the noon broadcast, the media finally realized that the world was in a state of crisis. I guess it took them a while to realize that these were real zombies in the big cities like New York and LA, I mean most people act zombielike in California and the people in New York are so blind to each other that they wouldn't notice anything out of the ordinary unless it came up and bit them, which is exactly what was happening.

The newscasters, all serious-faced, now expressed concern and they had tons of experts with expert opinions on exactly what was happening and why we suddenly had zombies in our midst. The expert testimonies varied from toxic waste, to aliens, to Armageddon, but the one thing everyone agreed on was that zombies were fictional monsters and were impossible in the real world. They were dead. The dead cannot rise mindless and attack the living. The only ones who did disagree were featured on the SyFy channel which then proceeded to run every zombie movie they could get their hands on.

I left after the dinner shift, which was very slow since it was winter and the nights were cold and grew dark early. By the time I caught a cab home, and cabs were scarce, the news was full of controversy.

I watched a film clip of the police taking flamethrowers to a cemetery in Chicago. It looked effective but up in the corner of the screen in a picture-in-a-picture box, media hungry rabble rousing representatives of every ethnic group in the city were screaming that this was a radical attack against the dead African American, Hispanic, Jewish, Catholic, Irish, Italian, Russian, you name it, population. I think there were more activists yelling about zombies then there actually were zombies at that point.

Every ethnic group in America was up in arms about the desecrations of their undead, although these same people were also screaming about the zombie problem that had to be taken under control immediately.

There was even a warning that undead animals were out in droves, only they seemed to eat their own species. All the same, the pet cemeteries seemed to be emptying out as well. Decaying and skeletal Fidos and Fluffys were returning to their human families.

The religious right screamed about the wrath of God and most members of the government were trying to deny a problem existed at all. Whatever and whoever, they all had a speculation, but it didn't really matter because zombies were eating everyone: Christians, Jews, Buddhists, and Muslims as well as Satanists and Atheists.

I turned off the TV and went to bed, comforted in the knowledge that mankind was as stupid as ever, and people only banded together to save the human race in the movies.

The next day the news was even bleaker. It seemed that the zombies were starting to travel in larger packs and that the newly dead were a lot quicker than their rotting companions. They were actually starting to attack people, individuals walking alone, homeless street dwellers, old age centers and teenagers who naturally insisted that they were invincible and ignored the warnings.

I gave up worrying about the world and wondered briefly if I needed to pay my mortgage on time or even ever.

Just in case the material world survived, I went to work, only I drove my old car that usually sat in the driveway ever since the gas prices went over six dollars a gallon. Just as I figured, parking was no problem that morning. No one was out, unlike the first morning of the zombie invasion.

I went in and looked at Lou and the two customers sipping coffee. "So you think the rush is over for today?" I asked. "Looks like the tips are going to be light."

Louie just shrugged and watched the wall-sized flat television. I followed his gaze. The zombies seemed to be growing in numbers. According to reports the flamethrowers at the graveyards seemed to be working a little, but the cops and fireman were getting spread thin, and a lot of zombies just got up and shuffled off the grounds, not bothering to use the roads and gates. Then, of course, there was the usual rioting and looting and, no surprise here, almost everyone suddenly rediscovered their religion.

One day into the undead crisis and life was settling into a new normal. Only a few people wandered in, although one guy came in with a gun and demanded money. I thought I would pass out when he burst through the door with his green Mohawk and leather jacket. He looked around quickly then screamed at Louie, "All your money! Now!"

Louie didn't even bat an eye. He reached toward the register and asked, "Whatcha need the money for, to pay off the zombies?"

The punk started to answer when his face went ashen. "Uh, no, don't need nothin'," and he backed out the door.

I turned to look at Louie and saw him holding a shotgun. "Puts his popgun to shame, don't it?" he said conversationally, then turned back toward the television. "Picked it up just in case. Even though it won't kill a zombie, it sure could slow the sucker down if I blow off its leg."

I nodded and glanced over at the only customer in the place, cowering in the last booth. "It's OK, Dan, you can get up now."

Dan stood and tried to act dignified, although it had to be difficult, since he had to get out from under the table and the front of his tan pants were wet. "That would make a great story, Lou," he said and took out his skinny little reporter's notepad. "Can get you on the front page for the morning edition."

Louie seemed to warm to the idea immediately. He turned to Dan and hit the off switch on the remote. "OK, ask away buddy, and for you, the coffee's free."

Overnight, Louie became a local star and an Internet sensation. He was a hero to the living who suddenly swamped the place, because, even facing what seemed to be the end of the world, people love celebrity. Dan, who had always hung around the restaurant anyway, became a regular, interviewing the customers because the newspaper gave him his own column called: *Living*.

After a month or so, the customers started to dwindle and the numbers of zombies on the streets began to increase. There'd been an intensive investigation that ruled out pollution, solar radiation, alien intervention, the wrath of God, and terrorist actions. Scientists finally announced the cause of the zombies.

Never-Dying Grass.

No solutions to the increasing numbers of the newly undead was offered, but at least we all knew now that it was once again the stupidity of the human race that brought about another ecological disaster, if you can consider the living dead an ecological problem.

Dan had a field day writing about Never-Dying Grass in his column. He went out and interviewed all sorts of sources, although he couldn't get a comment from the Green Seed Company. He never tried to interview a zombie, but he always talked like he was going to. He was just waiting for the right one to approach. It didn't matter that Dan was full of crap. He was scared and who could blame him. Nobody could talk to a zombie. They bite, and once bitten, you became a zombie, too.

Anyway, Never-Dying Grass had been somebody's brain child. A sure-to-sell idea ripe for developing and the Green Seed Company had jumped on it. With everyone spouting about going green to save the world, the seed company decided to develop a grass seed that only grew when it rained, stayed green, and self-fertilized whenever it did get wet, saving the world from fertilizer runoff.

Great concept. They sold it to cemeteries because it was so low maintenance and made even the shabbiest graveyards look well kept. Then they started selling it to parks and golf courses. Lucky break for the world that there weren't many dead people in those places. Because—you guessed it, whatever combination of rejuvenating fertilizers and chemicals resurrected the grass, it seeped into the ground and started resurrecting the buried dead.

What a mess. Once the grass was discovered as the culprit, it was torn out and destroyed. Too late.

It soon became obvious that the rotting zombies were falling apart, leaving pieces and limbs all over the streets. Their brains had turned from pudding to sludge that dribbled out of the openings in their heads. In the more intact members, the brain fluid leaked from eyes, ears, nose, and mouth, but, oh, the older bodies, they had so many holes that the brain cavity had to have emptied almost like a car radiator with a leak . . . either way, car radiator or zombie heads, they hemorrhaged green guts. But there were always fresher, newer zombies to take their place.

Life was trying to get back to routine only the mean streets were a little more dangerous. People carried weapons openly, lots of guns, flamethrowers, and gasoline soaked torches. Much of the zombie myths turned out to be pure fiction, but setting the living dead on fire was a sure way to make them permanently dead . . . forever.

After another few weeks, almost all of the original zombies were gone, rotted away to nothing, but the new zombies, the ones that were animated through contact, the ones that were never really dead to begin with, well they were somewhere in-between dead and not dead. They had that blank-faced stare, moaned and slobbered, but their limbs stayed intact, their eyes weren't turning to gooey bulging marbles, they had some of their coordination and dexterity, and worst of all, they had speed. These demons were quick and deadly. If they ever figured out how to band together as a thinking cohesive unit, mankind would be surely doomed.

I drove to work every day because I felt safer around Lou and the few regulars that still came in.

Then it happened. One day after the breakfast crowd, a term I use loosely, the door opened and in came three zombies, two pretty fresh and one who must have been a freshly dead original. They stood by the door and did nothing. One looked confused and then pained. "Huuuuh," he said and pointed at the counter.

"Give 'em a menu!" Lou whispered in a harsh raspy voice.

I stood my ground and stayed behind the counter.

Lou grunted with disgust and walked over to the dead trio. He held the cardboard menus out like a peace offering. The man who had made the sound slapped them out of his hand. Lou backed up a step, just out of biting range and said to me, "Set up three coffees and butter some of that leftover toast."

I stared at him like he was mad. I mean he had to be mad to even suggest feeding zombies.

"Do it!"

I did. I don't remember ever taking my eyes off the living dead customers, but somehow there were three set-ups with fresh coffee and toast. I pointed at the counter and to my shock, the small group walked slowly over and after many attempts to sit on the stools, they finally remained seated and upright. The moaner turned his dull eyes toward me and said, "Huuuuuh." He picked up the coffee cup with both hands and spilled it down his front. The other two followed his example and then they picked up the toast.

The rotting one shoved the buttered triangle into her cheek, tearing a hole in the soft, unresilient flesh. The other man managed to get some into his mouth and stopped dead. His features twisted into the most awful thing I think I have ever seen. Repulsed, I stepped farther away.

"MMMMM," he managed after a few tries. I stared at the spray of still dried crumbs that spilled out of his opened mouth and with a shudder, I realized he was trying to smile.

"Good, good," Lou said and smiled back. "See," he said turning to me, "business is picking up!"

I watched as the three struggled to get out of their seats and then I glared at Lou, "Business? Business? They're dead for the love of anything holy. What do you think, that they'll pay you? God, Lou, I can't go on like this, dead people are becoming our best customers, I'm broke, haven't made a decent tip in months, ever since this began, and you say business is picking up?"

Lou shrugged, "Baby, you just need to be adaptable."

Dan got up from behind the pinball machine, using a napkin to discreetly hide the wet stain spreading down his pants.

"Wow!" What a story: *Diner for the Undead!* Bet I make front page."

Lou beamed. "Somehow I'm going to get rich off of all this publicity. I can feel it in my bones! Rita, didn't I tell you the world wasn't coming to an end, just a new beginning!"

I shrugged and watched Dan writing in his notebook. "How come you don't use a hand held device to write with," I asked. "You look like Clark Kent."

Dan beamed at me, "Superman!"

"No," I said, remembering how Dan either left a quarter for lunch or stiffed me for the coffees that Lou never got paid for. "Clark Kent sums it up just fine."

Dan harrumphed and moved back to the booth he had inhabited before the zombies had eaten breakfast.

The next day, Dan did make the front page, but there was very little news except zombies doing this and zombies doing that and maybe an occasional living kitten or puppy rescued from their undead counterparts to lighten the load.

As Lou sat and admired the headline, five zombies entered the diner and headed for the counter. The original three and two buddies I guessed. I quickly got out the coffees and toast and Lou shouted from the kitchen to pick up an abandoned order of pancakes. The zombies moaned and grunted like they were in dead pig heaven.

When they finished, they shuffled off to do whatever it was that zombies do. Dan jumped up from the booth he'd been cowering in and started to follow them.

"Where do you think you're going?" I asked.

"To follow the story."

"Look, Dan, you really don't have a good nose for news, why don't you just stay and see if anyone else is coming in. Here," I said, "have a coffee and pie on the house."

Dan went back to his booth and waited the rest of the day to see if anyone else came in. Of course, after the story about zombies being welcomed, no one else set foot in the place all day.

Dan's next story was about the irrational fear of zombies hurting the economy.

Each day the zombies came, first five, then six, then they started coming in separate groups. We fed them, added meat to their plates, because a sated zombie was not a hungry zombie, and as the days progressed, attacks on the living in the blocks around the diner fell off.

It was a Saturday, not that the days counted for anything much anymore. A group of four zombies had just sat down to plates of day old tuna salad when Dan left his booth and walked up behind them.

Before I could shout stop, Dan had tapped one of them on the shoulder. "Say," he began. "Can any of you guys speak at all? I'd like to do—"

Before he could finish the sentence, the interrupted zombie turned and sank his teeth into Dan's head, ripping off a huge chunk of his face.

Dan cried out and fell to the floor, silent and still as the blood pooled around him.

I turned and threw up, then sank to my knees and cried. I didn't get up again until the zombies who had returned to their meal got up and left.

When I could finally stand again, I looked over the counter. Lou was nudging Dan with his toe. "Guess that ends the free publicity," he sighed and dragged Dan's body out to the curb. Then he came back in and called the zombie victim hotline. "Got a corpse on the curb," he said and gave the address.

I stood there, open-mouthed. How could Lou be so calm? Sure Dan was a jerk, but he was a fellow human being. Now he was destined to become either charred meat or reanimated flesh. I couldn't stand it. Tears were streaming down my face and I felt sick and totally confused.

Maybe the world really was beyond hope. I had not thought about giving up until that moment. I threw down my apron. I didn't even wait to see if the torch squad came and incinerated Dan. I just left, drove home, and locked myself in my nice safe boarded-up, steel-barred home.

I stayed there the next few days, but the walls just seemed to close in on me. With no place else to go, on the fourth day I went into work. Lou watched me enter and never said a word. After a few minutes the zombies started wandering in.

Some things had changed in the time I took off. When they finished eating one of the zombies got up and carried the dishes to the bus cart. Another got up and pushed a broom around the floor.

Lou smiled at me. "They just started working for their food. It seems that perhaps there is still a little humanity left in them or maybe they're just evolving."

"Evolving," I snapped. "They are freaking dead, Lou!"

Dan came shuffling in and sat. He tried to eat with only half a mouth, but he was still getting the hang of being reanimated. He smiled at me and said "Huuiii Riiitttaaa."

I felt my mouth just drop open and I had to physically push it shut.

Lou smiled, "As I said, a new generation, a little smarter. Evolution!"

After the last group wandered in, the zombie who had taken that first bite of toast all those weeks ago finished eating and turned to stare at me with those dull lifeless eyes. He gave me that god-awful twisted distorted smile.

"TPPPPPPPPPP," he sort of gurgled and got up to leave. He pointed at the hand he had left on the counter next to the plate.

I wanted to scream, but then I noticed a diamond ring on one of the gray swollen fingers.

"Tppppppppppppp!" he uttered again.

I nodded at my first tip in weeks and smiled back at my customer. Yes, evolution happens in many ways I decided, and pried the ring off the hand.

EVER WAITING FOR ROMEO

Juliet checked her phone, but no text. She looked at the clock. Only two P.M. and the mail didn't come until after two-thirty. Then she glanced at the calendar but it hadn't changed. Still February fourteenth.

She checked her cell phone again and almost jumped a foot when it starting vibrating in her hand. Juliet answered, gushing, "Oh Henry!"

"Seriously not Henry, but wanna tell me about him?"

Disappointment brought tears to her eyes. She blinked and said, "Oh hi, Cindy. Look I'm busy, so I'll call you later."

"But I'm downstairs. I'll be right up."

The line went dead and Juliet grimaced. Cindy may be her oldest BFF but she was incapable of keeping a secret, and Juliet was determined to keep Henry a secret until she was sure he was her one and only Romeo.

True to her word, Cindy was inside the small apartment before Juliet put the phone down. "Hey, Jill, you really need to lock your door. This is the asphalt jungle, the big city, not fifteenth century Verona."

Juliet frowned and snapped, "My name's Juliet,"

Cindy smirked, "Sure Jill, I forgot. But maybe you'd have a date for Valentine's Day if you'd just adapt to the twenty-first century, accept that you are Jill, and date a real guy, instead of searching for your fantasy true love."

"I keep telling you, I changed my name and I don't exactly see you getting ready for a romantic evening tonight."

"Well, it may not be what you consider 'romantic' but I'm seeing Tommy about ten o'clock tonight."

Juliet sniffed with disdain, "How special, a friend with benefits for Valentine's Day. You buying him roses?"

Cindy laughed and flopped on the couch. "As a matter of fact, he bought me a box of donuts last week. But, who's Henry, how'd you meet him, is he cute this time, does he have a job, how long you been dating and why'd you never mention him before?"

"Slow down or did you decide to take up journalism?" Juliet said and laughed too. "All right, but you gotta keep it a secret."

From the couch Cindy made the cross-her-heart sign and said, "Go on."

Juliet cleared her throat and asked, "Ok, do you remember Gregor Zroshky from the early 1970s."

"Uh, Jill, I mean Juliet, we weren't even born yet in the 1970s."

"But Gregor Zroshky was alive then. He was twenty-two when he made his only movie, the masterpiece, 'Zombies Evolutions: A Romeo and Juliet Story For The Dead at Heart'. It was the ultimate Zombie movie."

Cindy shrugged biting at a hangnail, "Then how come I never heard of it."

"It was so ahead of it's time that it never got released. Only a few pirated copies exist," Juliet said, her voice reflecting reverent awe. "And I have one, bought it at a horror movie convention."

"So what's this got to do with Henry? Was Gregor his father or something?" Cindy asked looking up from her nail.

Juliet smiled, "No silly, Gregor was a pen name. His real name was Henry Johnson."

"I see why he used a pseudonym? How positively common."

Juliet nodded, "Exactly!"

"I was being sarcastic!"

"Doesn't matter. Gregor was a legend and I found him on-line."

"God, he has to be older than the Cryptkeeper!" Cindy said and shuddered.

"He's only in his sixties."

"Juliet, your parents aren't even in their sixties!"

"Well, anyway, we've been emailing. And Cindy," Juliet paused for a dramatic moment. "Cindy, he's my Romeo. I've finally found my soul mate."

Cindy got off the couch and gripped Juliet's shoulders. "Listen to yourself! For once try to remember that Romeo and Juliet wasn't a fairy tale, it was a tragedy! They die in the end!"

Juliet pulled away. "I thought you were my best friend. I thought you'd be happy for me!"

Cindy sighed. "Jill, he's so old. You're in love with his movie, not him. Have you even met?"

"Well," Juliet hesitated, "Not yet. But I sent him a valentine with my picture."

The doorbell rang, both women turned toward the door. "I bet it's him!" Juliet shouted. "He texted he wanted to meet tonight. He's early."

Opening the door, her heart fluttered with disappointment. It was her postal delivery person.

"Just wanted to make sure you got this," he said. "Sorry."

She held out her hand and taking the envelope, recognized her own handwriting. She studied it and began to sob. "This has to be a mistake."

Cindy came over and looked at the red words stamped across the address, "Deceased, return to sender," she read. "Oh wow, Jill, I'm sorry."

Juliet sniffed a few times and then said, "It's a mistake, he's coming over tonight. He can't be dead. We're in love, just like Romeo and Juliet."

Cindy sighed loudly then muttered, "More like George Romero and Juliet." In a louder voice she said, "Come on Jill, you're been hoaxed by some sicko. Let's go out tonight together, I'll call Tommy and cancel."

Juliet stared at the dead letter in her hand. "Thanks, but I need to be alone now, see you tomorrow."

"You sure?"

Juliet nodded and sank onto the couch not sure what to feel. The emails had been so real, so loving. He had to be alive. He had too! She didn't even notice Cindy leaving or the room growing dark. She just sat mired in her despair. She didn't move until she became aware of a putrid, stench. It was so overpowering she started gagging. It was the odors of death and rot and was coming from the hallway right outside her door.

A gurgling, liquidy voice, gargled out "Juliet my love? I'm finally here."

Frozen with dread, she watched the doorknob jiggle. She was suddenly afraid that the man of her dreams, her soul mate, was a ghoul, a ghost, a zombie, or actually really dead.

Juliet wished she had listened to Cindy and locked the door.

But of course, just like in all the horror movies she enjoyed, she hadn't.

SPRING

BOBBY BUMPING

Brett yawned, taking his hands off the steering wheel to stretch. At five-thirty in the morning he had no oncoming traffic to worry about. In fact, he knew the only thing he had to worry about on this South Jersey back road was the occasional stray deer. He shuddered involuntarily and gripped the wheel again as he remembered how a deer had taken out the entire rear quarter panel of Tim's old Buick. If Bambi could do that to one of those gas guzzling tankers from the seventies, imagine what it could do to his tin and plastic import.

He straightened up and glanced at his watch. Working the night shift at the casino really screwed up his life, but the money was too good to complain. "So what if I don't have a social life?" he mumbled, stifling another yawn. "I'll get on the day shift soon. Just need to be patient."

Brett frowned as a fog seemed to roll in out of nowhere. One minute it was a clear night with daylight hiding just behind the eastern horizon, and the next he was in cream of mushroom soup. He tried to concentrate on the road but he was so tired. He blinked, fighting the urge to close his eyes, to rest them just for a moment. He slowed, then picked up speed. Better to get home faster than to be lost in this mess, he thought. After all, he knew that when he felt this exhausted the quicker he was safe in his own bed, the better off he'd be.

Suddenly, out of nowhere, there was a figure standing on the road in front of him. Brett practically stood on his brakes, but he knew it was a reaction way too late to do any good. He covered his eyes, but not before seeing the terror on the kid's face just before he heard that hideous thump-bump-crack. He was sure by the sound the teenager had bounced onto the hood and into his windshield.

Brett sat, his eyes covered, his foot still jammed on the brake and waited. He waited, hoping to hear a sound; a moan, a groan, a "hey buddy, watch where you're driving." But all he heard was the intolerable silence that made the slow motion time seem even slower.

After what felt like hours, Brett uncovered his eyes and shifted the car into park. The fog was lifting, he could see the smoky lake off to the left and the scrubby pines off to the right. He could hardly see anything straight ahead because the windshield glass was spider-webbed with cracks and a few streaks of red. "Oh no, no, no, no," he moaned, watching a red droplet roll down the glass, catch in a crack and fan out. "Oh, no, what have I done?"

He waited another minute, then two, hoping that something would happen, hoping that something would move, hoping the guy he just slammed into would get up and yell at him. Finally, he gave up hope and slowly undid his seatbelt. He gingerly opened the door, and waited. He didn't know what he was waiting for, but nothing happened. He thought about all those horror movies from his adolescent years and a new fear started to gnaw at him. He wanted to get out, see if he could help the kid, but he sat frozen. *What if he's not dead, but undead instead*, Brett wondered, fighting off an urge to shut the door and drive away. *What if he's going to grab my ankles as soon as I step out of this car and drag me off to the lake. Nobody'd miss me till tonight. Tim wouldn't even know I'm gone until his next day off or until he didn't find my rent check on the table at the end of the month. What if I've wandered into a real life slasher flick?* Brett laughed, a little too loud for his liking and perhaps a little to shrill. "I'm getting hysterical!" He shook his head and told himself, "Time to be a man about this!"

He stepped out of the car, hesitated a second, waiting to be grabbed and dragged, then slowly inched toward the front of the car. He saw the feet first, then the twisted legs and he knew that the kid was beyond help. As the head came into view, bent at a wrong angle, Brett suddenly lost control and threw up. He held the crumpled fender for support or he was sure he would have collapsed; his knees were so rubbery. "What do I do?" he asked the kid when he straightened up. "What do I do?"

He wiped at his cheeks and found them wet. He touched his tears, amazed that he was crying. "Like a baby," he mumbled and realized that was exactly how he felt at that moment. Like a helpless baby waiting for mommy or daddy to come make everything all better. But Mom and Dad were back in Washington and he was alone on a secondary road buried in the pines between two hick towns in Cape May County. The town he was living in didn't even have a police department, they probably didn't even have 9-1-1 dispatcher.

He walked backwards, unable to take his eyes off the body until it was blocked by the front end of his car. He slid back in and sat behind the wheel. After closing the door, he couldn't help but quickly glance at the backseat. Finding it clear of monsters and maniacs, he sighed then tried to figure out what to do.

He wished he had his cell phone on him, but he didn't.

What was he supposed to do, leave the scene of the accident and go look for a state trooper or stay here? He knew it was a crime to leave an accident but was he negligent to remain and wait for a passing car? He decided to stay, the kid was already dead, and he was guilty of hitting him. The sky was pink and the stars had retreated so he knew someone would be along eventually. He locked the door and closed his eyes. He knew sleep was out of the question so he sat there resting his eyes. And wondered about his life.

Would he go to jail? He doubted it, but he could lose his license. If that happened he'd have to move back to Absecon Island and depend on Jitneys again. No, he couldn't do that either. The rents were just too high in Atlantic City.

Meeting Tim had been a really lucky break. They had started out working the same shift and before he knew it they had become friends. One evening over drinks and a pizza, Tim said, "You know I've got a big house about forty-five minutes from here and since Dad died, I'm living there alone. Why don't you rent from me, we are going on different shifts next month so the place will be yours all day and mine all night. I'll make the price right!"

Brett sipped his drink, did some quick figuring and decided that even with the added mileage and wear and tear on his car this was a deal he couldn't afford to pass up. Of course, he hadn't figured on this kind of wear and tear, but it had worked out until now. He and Tim got along and had no problems sharing, and it was nice to have a big old farm house to entertain in the few times he had brought someone back with him.

He hadn't heard the approaching car, and jumped when he heard the knock on his window. He thought he was going to die on the spot his heart was racing so fast. It was full daylight and he saw Tim standing by the side of his car.

"Hey, Brett? What's the matter? Why you sitting here? Break down?"

Brett blinked for a moment and gathered his jumbled thoughts. That knock on the window scared him just about as much as the accident. "Tim! Boy, am I glad to see you! Go get some help!"

"What's the matter?"

Brett frowned with exasperation. *What was wrong with Tim?*

"Go get the cops, can't you see he's dead?"

Tim frowned back, "Who's dead?"

"The kid! What's the matter with you?"

Tim glanced around. "Nothing's the matter with me, what kid? Where?"

"The kid at the front of my car!" Brett yelled and pointed. He stopped and took in a quick breath. His windshield was intact, no cracks, no blood. Perfect.

He pushed the door open, knocking Tim to the side and rushed to the front of the car. The road was empty, no mangled body, no pool of blood. Only Brett's vomit on the side, showed that anything had gone on at all. "I …I … hit a kid last night, killed him."

Tim nodded, "Don't worry about it, let's go get a coffee back in town and we'll talk. Can you drive?"

Brett felt confused by Tim's lack of reaction but followed him to the coffee shop. They ordered and as they sipped coffee, Tim asked, "Foggy last night?"

Brett nodded, the coffee turning bitter as new fear gnawed at his guts. He was sure he wasn't going to like anything Tim had to say.

"You hit a teenage boy about seventeen or so wearing an orange and blue windbreaker and a red Phillies cap?"

Brett nodded again, taking a sip of water to try to get the bad taste of horror out of his mouth.

Tim smiled, "Well, Brett, you wouldn't have believed me before, but the kid's Bobby Watson. He died about twenty years ago, a hit and run accident on that road. Happened on a foggy spring night. It was a terrible thing, the talk of the town for months. Guy who killed him was never found."

Brett sighed, "So, every foggy night the ghost of the poor kid searches the road looking for peace, right?"

Tim shrugged. "I know it sounds like a cliché, but he's been hit repeatedly for years, always dies the same way, broken neck after bouncing off the windshield."

Brett sat and played with the coffee cup, spilling brown liquid onto the tabletop. "I'd laugh, except it happened to me. I killed a ghost!"

Tim grinned. "You know it's sick, but it's kind of a sport out here. They call it Bobby Bumping. People sometimes go out on a foggy night looking to hit him, it's the ultimate thrill."

Brett shuddered, "Some thrill! That was the worst feeling in the world. I thought I had killed another person!"

Tim grinned, "Yeah I know, but after the first few times, it's sort of fun."

Brett stared at his friend, "You've gone in for that sport?"

Tim reddened, "Well . . . yeah . . . you know, at first you don't want to, then the next thing you know, you see the kid in front of you and you know he's only a ghost and that you can't hurt him, and well . . . it just happens."

Brett felt a shiver run up his spine. It had been an awful feeling, but the adrenaline rush had been exciting and it was certainly safer than the rush you'd get from drugs or sky diving.

He shook those thoughts off. "I think I'm calling it a day. I need sleep. I'm just happy I didn't really hurt someone." He stood up to leave, shook his head and added, "Who'd ever believe that there really are ghosts? Really!"

A few nights later, Brett was driving home on the same road when the fog grew dense again. He knew that this was a common occurrence out here in the springtime when the temperatures change quickly near water but he slowed down to a crawl. He was on the lookout for poor Bobby Watson. Then, just as before, the kid was in front of him, terror frozen on his face. Brett hit the brakes and the car barely nudged the kid, yet Bobby flew onto the hood and smashed his face into the windshield.

Brett stared in amazement. He felt sickened, but not like last time. Now he understood. Whenever the kid appeared, he had to be hit. It was all obvious to him now. He didn't even get out this time, he just stopped until the shaking went away. He drew a deep breath and began to drive toward home. He waited for the crunch as he ran the kid over, but there was none. The minute he started forward, the cracked windshield cleared and everything was back to normal.

Brett grinned, despite the disgust he was feeling with himself, it was sort of fun in a morbid way. And he hadn't hurt anyone, in fact it was kind of his duty to hit the kid and send him back.

Before he realized it, Brett was the number one Bobby Bumper around. He never wanted to admit it, but he looked forward to the fog. *It's not like I go out and wait for the stuff,* he thought as the white mist started to rise off the road one morning. *It's just a fact of nature.* He looked around and saw that it was going to be a thick one, it was usually thickest if it started right before the dawn light. Brett felt high, He accelerated, looking for the solitary figure waiting to be sent back to purgatory.

"There he is," Brett yelled like a cowboy at the rodeo and floored the gas pedal. The little car roared as it rushed toward impact. "Yee-haw!" Brett bellowed as the body flipped onto his car and smashed into his windshield. "Bullseye!"

Brett drove the rest of the way home, feeling satisfied, like he'd just won at the table or had the best sex ever. He glowed with triumph, flavored with a small dash of guilt and a pinch of disgust.

Once in the house and out of the glow, he felt a full dose of remorse and disgust. "This really is sick! I'm going to give it up."

He nodded to himself, and decided that although the other route was a few minutes longer he wasn't going on the Bobby Road until the foggy season was over.

"I can be strong!" He said as he prepared for his day-lit night. "I don't need the thrills, I'm going to enjoy my life the way it should be lived. Maybe in a few months I'll move back to the island. I bet I can find a roommate to share an apartment."

He slept all day, satisfied that he was a strong-willed person. That night he took the long way to work and basked in his display of will-power. But as the night dwindled down to the wee hours and he clocked out and got into his car, he realized that he was hopelessly addicted to the sport. "I'm a weak piece of garbage!" he snarled. "Well, I'll do it just one more time. Yeah, just once more and then I swear I can give it up!"

Brett drove home on the Bobby Road. He felt disappointed when the sky remained crystal clear and there was no hint of a fog rising. Just as he gave up all hope of Bobby Bumping, a light mist began forming. Brett shouted and sped up. The mist thickened into a full sheet of sight-obscuring white and he drove even faster. If this really was the last time, it had to be the best.

The figure emerged, a dark blur in the fog, and Brett gunned the engine and surged ahead. His little car had never gone so fast. He braced for the impact and wasn't disappointed at all. The figure smashed into the car and crashed into the windshield so hard the glass actually broke. Brett hit the brakes, reversed, then accelerated forward so the figure would slide off and under his wheels.

But this time something was different. Brett fought off a shudder as the body crunched under his tires and the car bumped up and down.

"That's not supposed to happen," he mumbled, an uncomfortable feeling trickling through his nerves.

He slowed down to barely a crawl but kept going, and the trickling turned into a full buzz of fear when the windshield didn't fix itself.

The spider-webbed glass remained broken and he started shaking. *What's wrong*, he wondered, fighting the panic that was threatening to close off his windpipe.

"I couldn't have possibly hit a real person," he reassured himself just as the fog suddenly lifted and the sky to the east grew light with the sunrise. "Who'd be out on the road at this hour anyway?"

He slowed even more when he saw the orange flashers blinking in distress right up ahead. He stopped dead after he passed Tim's Buick sitting on the side of the road with the hood up.

And he started to cry when he saw in the new day's sunlight the small, crumpled, lump on the road reflected in his rearview mirror.

THE LAST PAGE

Loretta watched Mike pack his suitcase as anger and loneliness battled for dominance. Anger won again.

God, she always felt angry lately. *Is this what life had become, disappointment mixed with agonizing regret?*

She struggled to shrug off the depression that hugged her spirit like a killer bear. "How long will you be gone this time?" she asked and winced as the words "this time" came out coated with disgust.

Mike looked up from folding a shirt. "You know I have to go, it's my job. You think I enjoy traveling all the time. You think I'm doing this for fun?"

Loretta knew he hated traveling as much as she hated him going, but she couldn't control the words that poured out. "Hell, it's got to be better than being home with your family, better than helping with the kids and the house."

He slammed the suitcase closed, "Tell you what, Loretta, you find a decent job and I'll stay home with the kids. In the meantime, I've got a meeting upstate and as great as this conversation is, if I stay any longer I'll be late." He grabbed the bag, sighed and put it down. He turned and kissed Loretta lightly on the lips. "I'll try to get home day after tomorrow."

She stood motionless in the bedroom as she heard the door slam and then the car rev up and pull out of the driveway. Why, she wondered, why had she thought marriage and raising children would be her happy-ever-after? She'd had a job once, friends, and time to actually read a book. She'd been happy back then, but didn't realize all she had. No, she always wanted more. Now that she got what she thought was her heart's desire, she realized her heart's desire had changed, again.

She picked up the phone, put it down, then picked it up again. Holding it in her hand she stared at it, and finally punched in Mike's cell number.

He picked up right away. "Loretta?" he said in a cool tone.

She grimaced, if feelings could transmit over the phone her hand would be in danger of getting frostbite. "Hi," she said, trying to sound upbeat. "I just . . . I . . ." she stammered and then finished in a rush, "I just wanted to say have a good trip and . . . and I'm sorry. I may not act it, but I love you."

Silence for a double beat and then, "Uh, yeah, I'm sorry too . . . not about marrying you, but about all this traveling. I'm going to look for another job when I get back. You'll see, things will be different. Like the old days."

She started to reply, but he interrupted, "Cops ahead, gotta hang up. I love you, too, I really do."

Loretta looked at the silent receiver and smiled. He still loves me!

She thought about it. Maybe life can be better. Maybe she can learn to be happy again. "I love my family! Mike, the kids," she announced to the empty room. "I can be, no, I will be happy and satisfied!"

High from Mike's simple I love you, Loretta dressed for the day, not in the usual ratty sweat pants and tee shirt, but in a nice pair of jeans and one of those shirts that always hang in the closet waiting for the special event that never came.

She went outside and picked some tulips and put them in the good crystal vase. Then she vacuumed and dusted the house, put up a load of wash, and turned on the radio instead of the TV. She even made a real pot of coffee instead of a coffee pod and used the flavored creamer she saved for after dinner.

"I will live life to the fullest!" Loretta vowed to the family portrait on the wall. "Family life's like a merry-go-round, a long wait to get going, lots of ups and downs and sometimes a chance at that brass ring."

She stopped cleaning and rushed to her computer. "Hey, that was really deep." She typed her new philosophy onto her wall. "This should drum up a lot of comments," she said satisfied with her day and it was still morning.

The phone rang. Is it Mike? An accident? The school? She shrugged off the negative thoughts. She was happy; life was good. She'd finally turned the corner and now she was going to spend the rest of her life looking on the bright side. So why were those familiar dark feelings trying to creep in?

The phone stopped. After a brief hesitation, Loretta smiled and took another cup of coffee from the pot. She scolded herself, "Not everything is bad. The next time the phone rings, I'm going to win a million bucks!"

She sat and picked up the paperback she'd been trying to read for the last ten months. She turned to page thirty and began to read. By page thirty-four she remembered that she wanted to prepare the chicken for dinner.

Loretta sighed, put the book down for the millionth time and got up, her resolution to be a changed woman already fading.

The phone rang again. Loretta turned from cleaning the chicken to answer it.

She heard a breathless voice so jagged with emotion that she didn't recognize it at first. "Lori? Lori!"

"Marsy? Is that you?"

A sob, more heavy breathing and then, "Yes. Lori, it's horrible!"

Loretta rolled her eyes and smiled. She wanted to say, it always is with you, but instead said, "Calm down, what happened this time? Break up with what's-his-name?"

All she heard was shrill hysterical laughter and the phone went silent. Loretta went back to the chicken, thinking about Marsy. *What a drama queen, always on the brink of disaster*. She chuckled. "What a pair we make. Me always disappointed in everything and Marsy always living on the verge of hysteria. No wonder we're friends."

Not surprisingly, the phone rang again.

Loretta answered.

"Lori?" the voice was a whisper. "I only have a few seconds, we aren't supposed to call anyone."

"Seriously, Marsy, stop being so damned dramatic, what's wrong this time."

The whisper was a little louder. "Shut up and listen. It's the end of the world!"

Loretta couldn't help herself. "It always is with you—."

I mean it, Lori, they were drilling and using some new, top secret explosives . . . and something went wrong. Very wrong. It's going to start with earthquakes in about two hours and get worse really fast and then . . . and then it will be the end."

Lori stopped laughing. Marsy worked in some super classified lab developing alternative energy. There were always protests and rallies against them. People with placards exclaiming the end of the world. She and Marsy always laughed at them for being fanatics and crackpots. "Are you serious?"

"Yes, look, they'll kill me if they find me on the phone."

"Marsy, don't be so dramatic, just tell me what you're talking about."

"We are in lockdown and code red. Look, you're my best friend, I had to let you know. Get Mike and the kids and . . . I don't know, spend your last hours together. You're so lucky to have them. I wish, I wish I had someone to be with."

Loretta felt cold. She started shivering. Could this be for real? "Marsy, look, get over here. We're your family."

Sobbing. Loretta heard sobbing and knew that this time Marsy wasn't just full of shit. She heard voices, yelling, very loud popping, and then a male voice said into the phone, "Hello. Anyone there?"

Loretta didn't answer, just listened.

"Get a trace on this call."

Loretta dropped the phone grabbed everything off the table including her book and the empty coffee cup and swept it all into her pocketbook. She fumbled with her car keys and ran to the garage. Two minutes later she was driving aimlessly wondering what to do.

She looked around and pulled into a crowded parking lot. She felt safe there, but just for a moment. How safe can I be if the world is really going to end in a few hours, she wondered.

The world was going to end! Everything she ever knew and loved would vanish forever. Everyone would be dead. "Oh, my poor, poor babies! Mike! My parents!"

Hot tears rolled down her cheeks. Loretta wondered what was happening. Was Marsy lying, making things worse than they were. She'd made mountains out of molehills before. But that man's voice, so very ominous and those noises, like the gunshots she'd heard on TV. Had they killed her best friend?

Loretta's teeth began to chatter and she felt like she was going to be sick. She opened the door, threw up, then just sat motionless. Her life, as crappy as she had felt it to be, was now the most valuable thing in the world. Her children, her babies, were about to die and all she could do was sit in her car and cry. So much loss, she didn't know what to do or where to start. She was the only person outside the government agency that Marsy had worked for who knew that everyone on Earth, every living creature was going to be gone in just a few hours.

She couldn't stop crying. Poor Marsy, but then again, if Marsy'd been right, maybe she was the lucky one, a quick death, if . . . if she were dead at all. But Loretta knew deep down, Marsy really was dead, murdered in the name of security. "I've . . . I've got to do something!"

She struggled to think past the panic and fear. She kept hearing those shots and that man's voice. She wanted to mourn for what was to come, to grieve for everything that was about to be lost, but it was just too big, too overwhelming.

She thought about calling a TV station and telling them what was going to happen, but what was the point. By the time they acted on it, if they believed her at all, it would be over. She'd only accomplish panic, worldwide hysteria.

No, Loretta decided. This knowledge was a curse, a curse she couldn't share with anyone. "Why'd she ever call me?" she said and wept into her hands.

She heard that man's voice in her head again and it cut through her fear and grief. He'd said get a trace on that call. "Ohmygod, maybe they're going to come after me!" It didn't matter that the world might end shortly, she had to get away from him now. No matter what, she didn't want to die, not as long as she could live.

"I'm sorry." she said, just to hear a voice. "I've been such a jerk, a fool. Why couldn't I enjoy life? I had Mike, the kids. Oh, I wish I could fix this."

She began half-laughing, half-crying. "Too late now."

But was it, was it too late? Was it ever too late? She remembered sitting in a dorm room smoking pot and having one of those deep conversation that young people have. "What would you do if you knew the world was going to end tomorrow?" someone had asked.

Loretta tried to picture herself a decade and a half ago, innocent of what life was really about, discussing great philosophical topics, solving the world's problems. Usually, she just mellowed out, let the pot take her to her inner place until someone brought out the food. But that discussion had caught her interest.

"I'd eat until I threw up and then I'd eat some more," the anorexic girl from two rooms down had said.

Someone else exclaimed. "I'd rob a bank and spend all the money I could before the end."

"I'd go to India and see the Taj Mahal."

"I'd get laid. A lot!"

"I'd max out my credit card."

"I'd run home and spend the end with my parents."

Loretta laughed, "You're all so wrong. It's all going to be over, so, whatever you do, well, it just won't matter because you can't change a thing."

"Yeah," someone interrupted her. "If you're so smart what would you do?"

She said, "I'd get stoned out of my gourd and jump off a bridge. Hell, what's the point of prolonging the inevitable, the agony of waiting for the end you know is coming. Make it quick and clean and die on your own terms."

The conversation went on for a while longer with half the crowd buying into Loretta's idea of taking control of destiny and the other half waxing sentimental or just silly.

Now she looked back at that conversation and knew she'd been wrong, they'd all been wrong. *What you would do*, she decided as she sat in that parking lot with knowledge she never should have been given, *was grab life and hold onto it, try to change destiny, fight for every last breath, and if all else failed, do what you could to make those last minutes matter.*

Loretta suddenly felt energized. The fear was still there, but she had a plan. She couldn't let that murderous bastard find her or her kids. Just in case they actually traced her line, she was way ahead of them because she was here and not home, and as ironic as it seemed, time was on her side. She tore out of the parking lot, ran a red light, a ticket didn't matter anymore, and pulled into the no-parking zone at the school. She ran up the stairs two at a time, burst into the office and not even waiting for her turn at the front desk, and yelled. "I need Janie and Timmy Bradley now."

"Mrs. Bradley, if you could just wait a minute."

"Don't have a minute, call them down now! I'm signing them out!" Loretta yelled again. She grabbed the pen and signed the sheet, then took off down the hall to their classrooms. She burst into one, then the other, and grabbed her children, ignoring the protests from the teachers.

"Boy, Marsy had better be right or there is going to be hell to pay tomorrow," she muttered as she dragged her children to the car, buckled them in and took off.

Janie was crying. "What's wrong, Mommy?"

Loretta looked at herself in the mirror. She looked like hell. The make-up she'd applied earlier when she'd vowed to be a new woman had run from her tears. her face was puffy and splotchy, her eyes red. But she smiled at her children. She was feeling better, stronger, a woman with a goal. Sure, she realized, the fear would return, but for now, action was enough to keep her going.

"One of Mommy's friends died, not anyone you knew and I was feeling sad so I decided I needed you guys to help me cheer up."

"Oh, Mommy, I'm sorry." Janie said and stopped crying, after all it wasn't her world falling apart.

"Yeah, we can do that," Timmy said with eight-year-old bravado.

51

"We're great at making you happy!"

Loretta looked into the rearview mirror at her two children, her boy and her girl, and realized that they were great at making her happy she'd just been too busy being unhappy to know it.

"Tell you what, let's go to the store and get some new clothes, then we'll buy lunch and eat by the ocean."

"But it's April."

"Doesn't matter, you can still build a castle in the spring."

Loretta picked out the most expensive jeans and jackets for all of them, and new athletic shoes as well. She smiled briefly as she remembered that long ago college conversation and thought, *what the heck, charging up a storm is a good idea.*

They went to the market and got sandwiches, chips, cupcakes, a giant bag of chocolate candy, the kind you ate by the handful and sodas full of sugars and chemicals. She picked up one last item that the kids didn't notice, put it in her pocketbook and they headed for the shore.

Janie asked for music on the radio but all that was on was the news, and it was bleak. Earthquakes were happening everywhere, most of them small but every continent was experiencing them. Loretta sighed, the overwhelming waves of sadness were returning. It was true. There was nothing she could do to change it.

She continued driving. *What do you do when you know the world is going to end?*

She thought, *you go on living until it does.*

"Here we are!" she exclaimed with loud, false excitement. She opened the trunk because she knew she'd never emptied it from the summer. "Get out the buckets, shovels, and beach chairs and let's go have that picnic."

The day was chilled and cloudy and they were the only ones there. As they settled down near the water's edge, Loretta opened the candy, gave the kids large bottles of soda, and she removed the lid on her café mocha topped with extra whipped cream. "Go play," she said and shooed the kids off. She thought about calling Mike, having him on the line as the end came, but decided that was silly. They'd said, I love you when it mattered. What more could be added to that?

She sat in her beach chair and sipped her coffee as she popped candy-coated chocolates into her mouth. She could feel the tremors starting and saw the sand jumping. As she looked out at the water, the sun burst through the clouds making the rapidly receding ocean sparkle like a million diamonds.

She thought about calling the kids to her, to hold them, but then decided why scare them, they're happy playing in the sand.

She sighed and thought, *what do you do when you know the world is going to end? You go on living until it does.*

Then she reached into her purse, opened the pack of cigarettes she had slipped in there at the market and lit the first one she'd had in a dozen years. As she inhaled the smoke into her lungs, enjoying the sensation despite the waves of dizziness, she opened that book she'd been trying to finish. She ignored the bookmark, opened to the end and began to read the last page.

THE QUEEN

Melinda, licking the cotton candy crystals from her fingertips, wished she were enjoying herself. The sky was ominous, the midway overcrowded, and the pain in her stomach was growing worse by the minute.

Why'd she come here anyway, she wondered, and fingered the car keys in her pocket. She dreaded the circus and everything it represented and yet when she found the free ticket in her mailbox she knew she had to come. After years of avoiding the big top, she found herself here.

She studied the giant full-colored posters lining the corridor created by tents and the little trailers selling food. Faded painted acrobats swung from trapezes, leotard-clad men carrying long balancing poles were frozen for all time gingerly stepping their way across the high wire, young women in sequins held hoops for performing dogs probably long dead. Every poster a cliché, and yet, and yet, something eerie and not quite human surrounded those images.

Melinda quickly averted her gaze and stood in the middle of the midway, staring at the ground, trying to decide whether to go home or stay and try to discover why she needed to be here. That was when she felt the first raindrops like a gentle tap on her shoulder. She spun around and realized no one had touched her, it was just the soft drops of an April shower. But then the sky opened up and the rain fell all around her in skin-soaking sheets. A flash of lightning lit up the area, then plunged it into a dull, dark premature nightfall. Without thought, she rushed into the striped tent to her immediate right. She dashed through the flap and almost ran into a woman with caked make-up and large rings on every finger.

The woman's wrinkled face registered instant recognition. "It's you!" she said. "At long last, it's you!"

Taking an awkward step back, Melinda shuddered. The old, carnival gypsy was smiling through ruby red lips and pointing at her. "It's you!" echoed in her head as she backed out of the tent and stood in the rain for a full minute before realizing that she was soaked.

Melinda began to shiver even though the late afternoon was warm. Teeth chattering, she looked around, but couldn't get her bearings. Striped tents were everywhere and she entered one at random, making sure it wasn't the one she had just fled.

The flap swished closed behind her and her eyes slowly adjusted to the dark, musky interior. She could see racks of costumes: spangled leotards, silly clown suits, short red jackets, and a long ringmaster's coat. Melinda relaxed and grabbed a deep rich purple velvet jacket, a jacket that fit so perfectly it seemed to mold itself to her and exude warmth. In a few minutes she stopped shivering and in a few more, the dark and the new-found warmth lulled her to sleep.

A deep sleep, filled with images of circus life: animals, clowns, gypsy fortune tellers, trapeze artists, clowns, elephants, clowns, and faceless people who wanted her and frightened her, yet, were not ominous. She woke, feeling uneasy and confused. She tried to think, but couldn't get all the visions out of her head. Why'd she come to the circus anyway?

Oh yes, she remembered, to prove to herself that there was nothing to fear. She'd never been to a circus, hated playing big top with the other kids as they hung upside down on swing sets. She'd always been afraid of the big top, ever since she was a little kid, moving from foster home to foster home.

She felt the heavy weight of disappointment. She hadn't defeated or even confronted her demons. She left the dark protection of the costume tent and decided to sneak away before anyone discovered her.

Everything was so quiet, no noise filtered in from outside, no laughter, no midway barkers calling to the crowd, no ringmaster's demands to look left or right or center ring, no calliope of tinny music. Just silence, silence as thick and impenetrable as the darkness enveloping her.

The midway was closed, the rides still, the animals asleep. It felt as if she were the only living soul at the circus. She looked over the midway, the food concessions closed up tight and the games of chance silent. She saw a slit of light coming from the tent she had run into the first time, the fortune teller's tent. Why had that gypsy acted like she knew her?

Gathering up all her courage and ignoring the weakness in her knees, Melinda went over, lifted the flap and walked inside.

The gypsy was seated at the table with two cups of tea and cookies. "Come and sit, dear. I'm sorry I frightened you earlier. It was just the shock of seeing you again. We'd almost given up hope, even though the cards foretold you'd be back."

Melinda took the chair. The tea looked inviting and she was hungry. "You know me?"

The gypsy laughed, "Yes, of course, dear. Do you know you?"

Melinda shook her head. "No," she whispered, "No, I don't really know me at all. I don't have a past."

"Yes, dear, you do. How much do you remember?"

"Living in foster homes but not knowing anything more about me than my first name."

"Well, Melinda," the gypsy said in a soft, kind voice. "Here take my hand."

Fearfully grasping the ring-covered, red-nailed hand that looked like a vicious talon but felt like soft velvet, Melinda was suddenly engulfed in images. Memories. This was her home. She tried to remember why she'd run away, but all she could recall was the clowns chasing her, clowns hunting for her, all these years, hunting for her. Wanting her.

She let go and gasped. "I remember! I ran away. Ran from all of you! Oh, the clowns, the clowns. I've got to get out of here!"

The gypsy reached for her hand. "No, don't try to leave. You're home now."

Melinda jumped up and ran out. She saw them then, the clowns, lurking, hiding in the shadows. She had to get away. She ran, no one followed, but she could sense them all around her. So many clowns, why would such a small circus have so many, many clowns. She ran down the midway, blind to everything. Searching for a way out, she felt them closing in, drawing their circle tighter.

A doorway! Without thought, she ducked inside to find herself surrounded by herself. She reached out and touched glass. The house of mirrors! She ran, blindly bumping into glass walls, confusing herself, losing herself. She was everywhere, reflecting back at herself, hundreds of Melindas.

She sank to the floor and wept. What did all this mean?

She heard them, saw them wandering the maze in search of the real her. There were hundreds, no thousands of clowns surrounding her as they reflected endlessly in their quest.

"If I just stay still maybe they'll never find me," she whispered.

"Ah, Melinda, they will find you. They have, too, they need you to come home." Melinda looked up and saw the gypsy standing before her. The older woman smiled and held out her hand. "Come, it's time to come home and take your rightful place."

Tears streaming down her cheeks, Melinda took the old hand and suddenly another memory flooded in. "Momma, Momma!"

The gypsy smiled, and her once ominous face was suddenly warm and caring. "Oh Melinda."

"Oh Mother … Momma, I ran away … I was scared … terrified. I didn't want the responsibility. I was … I was just a dumb little kid. Then I forgot, I think I wanted to forget."

"I know, Melinda, it is hard to accept who we are, who we sometimes must be. A hard road for a sensitive child. My poor baby. All those years, I've missed you."

"Me too, Momma, I got lost and didn't know how to get home. Melinda smiled and hugged her mother. The last puzzle pieces fell into place. She was a part of the circus world, an important part never known by the mundane world.

She looked down and with a shaking hand, lifted a bright red nose from the floor and pulled it over her small one. A perfect fit.

She was Queen of the Clowns, clowns the world over would soon hear of her return and all would once again be right. That was what had frightened her as a child, made her run away. Too much to handle.

"That's right, you are our queen." the clowns all shouted in a roar as they filed out into the night, following her. "Long live the queen."

Melinda crossed the midway and paused to face them. They bowed. Turning, she continued on. She came to a huge golden tent and entered. The clowns followed her, then the rest of the circus family entered as well. She walked to the end, to the throne, her throne. She took the gold crown covered in garish, brightly colored jewels from the velvet seat and placed it on her head.

Smiling at her throng of cheering subjects, Melinda sat, picked up her scepter and squeezed the bright orange rubber bulb at one end. As the horn blared out ARRUGAH she laughed, knowing she was finally home where she belonged.

MOTHERS' DAYS

Confused, lightheaded and . . . well, very, very confused. Barb stared at the magazine in her hand. *Where did this come from*, she wondered, absently thumbing through the pages.

Lethargy enveloped her and she struggled to think through a brain seemingly filled with cotton. Her life. Her life was so fuzzy, shadowy. Like a resume, just words.

Name: Barbara Cross
Age: 26
Husband: Tony
Married: eight years

She smiled with relief and said aloud, "Oh yes, that's right and most important, I'm Kenny's mom. She hesitated for a brief moment, then with the confusion sweeping back over her, she placed her hand on her abdomen before continuing. "And I'm expecting again."

She stopped and a shiver ran along her spine like a tiny spider. "I am?"

She shifted her gaze down to her protruding tummy that was stretching the fabric of her T-shirt. "I don't remember being pregnant! That's something I certainly shouldn't, couldn't forget."

She pushed herself up from the wooden kitchen chair and grabbed the baby intercom receiver from the counter. Rushing out the back door, crossing the withered lawn that joined the identical townhouses, she softly knocked on her neighbor's door.

"Phil, Phil, I'm losing my mind!" she gasped breathlessly as soon as the door was opened.

"Barb! Slow down and catch your breath," her neighbor Phyllis said, and stared at Barb's belly with a perplexed expression. She started to say something, but stopped, shook her head ever so slightly, then smiled. "Now what's this about being crazy? No, wait," she said holding up her hand. "Let's have some coffee and talk. After all, it might be a long discussion because all mothers are insane. Why else would we be mothers?"

"No time. Kenny's still napping and I hate to leave him alone."

Phyllis poured two cups of coffee and gently forced Barb to sit. "You have the intercom right in your hand and these walls are paper thin. Relax!" She flashed Barb a sympathetic smile as she ran her hand through her short, platinum-blond hair.

Barb smiled back at this woman who'd been her best friend for years. But, how many years, she thought briefly then let it pass. "I'm pregnant!" she said, tears welling up in her brown eyes.

"You certainly are," Phyllis laughed. "Been that way for months."

"How many?" Barb asked.

"Huh?" Phyllis said, blinking her pale, winter-blue eyes.

"I said how many months?"

"Oh, let's see," Phyllis said. "I don't know, a couple of months. Don't you remember how far along you are? When's your due date?"

Wanting to scream: I have no idea, Barb opened her mouth and replied, "July tenth, which makes me about five and a half months."

Where'd that come from, she wondered, her throat growing tight. Struggling to swallow, she forced a deep breath down the constricted passageway. *I know I wasn't pregnant this morning, I just know that I wasn't! Could wanting something cause it to spontaneously happen, she thought. Or am I really losing my mind? Why can't I remember anything correctly anymore?*

Her thoughts jumbling and colliding, she asked, "Where'd you go to high school, Phil?"

"... Harrison High," Phyllis answered after a moment's hesitation.

"Remember much about it?" Barb pressed.

"Why … uh… sure," Phyllis answered, sounding unsure of herself. "Why all the questions about my past?"

Barb paled as she whispered. "I don't think I have a past at all!"

"What do you mean?"

"I feel like I only have right now to keep. I don't know how to explain it, just that I feel like I've never had a life at all," Barb said with a shudder. "My memories are so . . . so one dimensional. Like they've been handed down over generations, you know, like a racial memory. Somehow I don't think I'm the original me!"

"We all feel that way at times, especially when expecting a child," Phyllis said, and gently laid her hand on Barb's shoulder. "It's all right to be confused, your whole system is completely out of whack from nurturing that life within you."

"I . . . I guess maybe you're right, I'm just tired and out of sorts," Barb said, trying to convince herself. "Why, I remember being pregnant," she blurted out as a sudden explosion of information filled her head. "Kenny's wanted a brother for a while now."

The air was abruptly pierced by a shrill, high-pitched cry, "Mommy, me up!"

Phyllis jumped up and headed for the stairs. "Gotta get Kathleen, be right down."

"Don't rush," Barb said getting up. "I've got to get home anyway. Kenny will be awake soon, too. See you outside later if it stays sunny."

Shivering in the chilly late March breeze, Barb walked slowly, trying to dredge up clear memories of her youth. All she could really recall were words with fuzzy mental images: cheerleader, proms, braces, living in an apartment over a corner market, dating Tony all through high school.

"What's wrong with me?" she whimpered as she entered the warm sanctuary of her kitchen and shook off the early, spring cold that seemed to creep inside her. "Why do I feel like a carbon copy of myself?" Before she could worry any further she heard the familiar sound that signaled the end of her quiet time.

"Mom, Mom! I had a accident."

"Oh, damn," Barb groaned. "Almost three stinking years old and he's regressing. I wonder if he'll blame it on his imaginary friend again. I swear he thinks she's real!" A shiver crawled down her back all the was to her toes and she felt like she was going to remember something. Something really important. "Friends . . . friends," she mumbled, trying desperately to bring the nagging but elusive thought into focus.

"Mom! I'm up!"

Feeling frustrated, feeling like her entire existence seemed to be only to tend to the domineering king of her existence, Kenny, she lost her grasp on what she was trying to remember. Sighing, she went upstairs to change the wet sheets.

She entered her child's room and frowned. "Kenny, big boys don't go pee-pee in their pants."

"I didn't," the chubby red haired toddler replied, showing his teeth in a sweet smile.

"Oh, Kenny," she snapped, disgusted with motherhood. "Of course you did!"

Starting to whine in a nerve-grating, high-pitched voice, Kenny simpered, "I didn't, my friend did it, she was in the crib with me."

Once amused by his imaginary friend, Barb now loathed this mysterious instigator. "All right," she said, and lifted Kenny out of the crib. She ignored his wet clothes and hugged him close to her, wishing she could remember things clearly.

The little boy squeezed her back. "You're a good mommy!"

She smiled and set Kenny down, "I love you, my bestest boy in the whole world. Let's get changed, then you can go outside and play with Kathleen."

An hour later, the two children were side-by-side in the tot-lot down the block. Phyllis and Barb sat on the bench next to them and tried to hold a conversation around constant interruptions.

"I think Kenny's imagination is sometimes too advanced," Barb said. "He has more excuses for his actions and all of them involve a girl who doesn't exist. You know, sometimes I get frightened by this friend of his. He acts like he can really see her."

Phyllis started to say something in return, but was cut off by Kenny. "Mom! Mom! I need some juice," he demanded from his seat in the sand box. "And so does my friend!"

"All right, I'll run home and get two cups of juice for you and

Kathleen," Barb said, giving in to his demands instead of telling him to wait like she really wanted to do. She just didn't have the energy to put up with another tantrum.

"Noooo!" he shrieked, his face turning red and clashing with his orange hair. "Not Kat-leeen! For my other friend!"

Barb cringed, hating this intruding non-entity more with each mention of it.

"Kathleen has an imaginary daughter living in our closet. I guess we all have to get used to it," Phyllis said interrupting Barb's thoughts. "Anyway, don't bother about Kathleen's drink. It's chilly, we're going home now."

Phyllis turned to the two-and-a-half-year-old on the sliding board and called, "Kathleen, come on, honey, time to go home."

The little girl began to whimper. "No, don't want to go home."

Phyllis sighed and went over to grab Kathleen's hand. "Come on, it's too cold. Time to go in and watch television."

Barb watched the all too familiar scenario as Phyllis's child pulled her hand away and screamed, "No, no, no, I no want in!"

Phyllis stopped smiling and picked up the kicking, squirming toddler. "Stop it right now, young lady. I'm in no mood for this." She softly smacked the child's diapered bottom as she snapped, "We're going home, now."

As the two white-blond haired figures left the playground, Barb smiled grimly as Kathleen wailed those oh-so-familiar words. "Bad mommy, you a bad mommy! I don't love you anymore!"

She wondered why words could hurt so much.

Kenny stopped playing and came over to Barb. He rubbed her thigh like she were a good pet and said, "Kat-leeen was crying, her mommy was mean, but I love you. Can we have a drink now?"

Barb stood up, took Kenny's hand and led him past all the look-alike tract homes. She noted, as if for the first time, that the only real differences in the houses were the flowers and shrubs starting to decorate the front yards. When they got to the bland, tan house with the yellow daffodils bending in the stiff breeze, they went inside. After all, Kenny and his friend needed their damned drink.

The next morning, the weather warmed and the temperature soared into the low seventies. As she joined the other mothers from the neighborhood at the playground, Barb took her place on the bench next to Phyllis. Glancing at her friend, she started to smile, but frowned. "You look different today, change your hair style?"

Phyllis smiled and answered, "Nah, just didn't have time to do anything with it this morning." She swept up her long, dark blond hair with one hand and added, "Never have the time anymore, but then that's motherhood. I'd cut it short, but Kathleen loves my hair long, she likes to play with it. And you know, the kids always get their way."

Barb wanted to insist that the change was something more, but when she stared into Phyllis's robin-egg blue eyes, she felt that flood of memories rush in again, memories that told her Phyllis was the same as always, Phyllis was correct. She realized she was just being silly.

"Yeah, they always do get everything they want, don't they," she agreed and thought about her dream last night. It had scared her so much, yet, she couldn't remember it clearly. Just snatches . . she'd been a kid . . . her mother vanished, melted, then her father . . . she had friends, actually the same friend repeated over and over and over again like an image caught between two mirrors. What a nightmare!

"Phyllis, did you have an imaginary friend?" Barb asked, nebulous memories nagging at her again.

Phyllis smiled, "Sure did, named her Patsy. My mom told me all about her. I guess I was too young to remember."

"So did I, I think," Barb said. "I've been having strange dreams about a friend. I don't know why, but it upsets me to remember her."

"Don't dwell on it then," Phyllis said. "I try not to upset myself with nonsense. Being a mom is upsetting enough."

They sat and watched their children and Barb squinted her eyes until all she could see were blurry shapes. *Am I seeing an aura of something?* She shifted her gaze to look at the other toddlers in the playground. Yes, yes, she seemed to be seeing something some of the time. About a quarter of the kids appeared to have something shimmery and pale beside them.

Her eyes started to burn and she could almost swear that the children with the auras were looking back at her, watching her.

She shuddered, looked away, and shut her eyes. Blinking a few times she looked around at the normal scene around her.

"Don't you think it's a little weird that we both had imaginary friends and now our kids do too?" she asked.

Phyllis shrugged and thumbed through her gossip magazine. "Maybe it's hereditary."

Barb stared at her friend like she had said something truly profound. "Maybe it is," she said slowly, something nagging at her, trying to crawl to the front of her brain. She opened her mouth, the words almost there--then they were gone. She sat not uttering a word and tried to avoid staring at the playing children.

She spent the rest of the day like all others, continually shifting her emotional gears between anger and amused devotion to her child. But she also had to contend with something new: fear. Although Kenny didn't leave her any time to think about the things that were eating at the edges of her memory, she still maintained that feeling of discomfort bordering on terror.

By Kenny's bedtime, Barb was beyond exhausted. Once again, Tony was on an overnight business trip, leaving her with total responsibility for the care of their child.

"When the next one comes, things are going to be different," she muttered, angry at her life. "Tony's going to have to help more."

Struggling to get Kenny to stay in his crib, she finally tucked him in and kissed his forehead. "I love you, Kenny. Now stop this nonsense and go to sleep. Mommy's too tired tonight!" she said as she turned on the nightlight and left the room.

Back in her bedroom, across the hall, she ignored the begging cries and collapsed on her bed. "Ah shit!" she mumbled. "I'm too tired to keep this up."

Somehow during the day, her nagging fear had changed, had shifted and became more. The idea of changing, of being reborn over and over again, of being versions of herself, wouldn't go away, rather it was growing into irrational horror. She shivered under her comforter, and her dream of the night before began to suddenly crystallize. Her mother, hands out imploring, begging. Then she became wavy, indistinct, as someone touched her, someone . . .

"Mom! I'm lonely! I need you! Now!"

She stifled a scream as Kenny's voice ripped the vision away.

"Not now, Kenny! Go to sleep!" she yelled back. She'd lost it, the memory of the dream. She'd felt so close to getting it, to understanding, and now it was gone. *Had life ever been calm and happy,* she wondered, looking at the smiling people in the photographs that peppered the walls.

"Don't be a bad mommy! Come here!" he yelled then seemed to give up.

He became quiet and Barb started to relax. *Maybe now I can figure out what it is that's been nagging at me,* she thought. She got out of bed and headed for the bathroom when Kenny cried out, "Mom, Mom!"

"What now!"

"Mom, I don't need you anymore, my friend said she will make me not lonely now. She's a good friend!"

"Good!" Barb called as she finished and returned to the beckoning bed. Propped up with several pillows, under the toasty comforter again, Barb strained to listen to Kenny talk to his friend. Suddenly, she thought she heard another voice.

She pushed her swollen body up off the soft, comfortable mattress, and tiptoed into her child's room. She was scared, legs weak, heart beating like bat wings. At the doorway she froze and stared. Sitting Indian style on the floor, Kenny was playing with a faintly translucent little girl with long brown hair and Kenny's facial features.

Hand to her mouth, Barb gasped. Fear cut off her breath and something else wouldn't let her catch it again. Her chest began to ache.

The two children looked over at her and the girl smiled. "You ready, Kenny?" she asked.

"Yes," Kenny answered.

Barb stared, terror and lack of oxygen freezing her to the spot. The girl grew solid and started to change shape. This was familiar . . . so very familiar. She knew she had experienced this before.

"NO!" she screamed voicelessly. "I won't let it happen again. This is my life!" But instead, swaying and dizzy, Barb crumpled to the floor, unable to breathe. "Wait . . ." she wheezed. "Wait . . ."

The memories came in a cold gush; this friend, Kenny's friend had once been hers. "Mizzy?" Barb choked. "Why . . . are . . . you . . . doing . . . this . . . to . . . me?"

The girl, now a woman, looked at Barb. "Because I have to. You know that."

Tears ran down Barb's cheeks and she nodded. She knew now that it was the way it had to be. Mizzy belonged to Kenny now, or rather Kenny and Mizzy belonged together.

Until the baby comes and takes Mizzy away.

And then Kenny will forget. They all forget.

Kenny came over to stand above her and smiled his sweetest, most innocent smile. "Mommy, Mommy, I told you I don't need you anymore. Go away, I have my good mommy now!"

Gasping, unable to speak or take in air, Barb's world grew dim, dark, and blurred at the edges. *Now I understand*, she thought with her last ounce of failing reason. *I was once real, but how many Barbs ago was that? Which copy am I? How many times have I been . . . renewed?*

The girl, now a pregnant woman, come over to Barb and gently touched her face. Barb felt her memories and her very essence being sucked away. With her last conscious thought, she couldn't help but feel pity for her new self.

Mizzy smiled Barb's smile and whispered in Barb's voice, "Don't pity. Most never remember."

After a long moment, after Barb had been totally absorbed, sucked away, all was quiet. Still.

Then Kenny took his new mommy's hand and said, "You will be a good mommy, won't you?"

Barb shook her head and wondered what she'd just been doing. She shrugged off the moment's confusion, squeezed her son's little hand and answered, "Oh course I will, I always am."

UNCONDITIONAL LOVE

"**Y**ou found it in our cellar?" Janet asked, fighting off a shudder.

"Yeah, Mom," Buddy said in a breathless rush. "You know … where the cellar stops and that dirt shelf goes the rest of the way under the house!"

Janet frowned, "I've told you not to go into the crawlspace. It could be full of rats or something."

"Ah Mom, come on, rats? I haven't seen a rat since we moved. Anyway, nothing happened except I found this locked crate down there. Can we open it?"

"I … don't … know," Janet said, hesitating. As much as she loved this old, ramshackle row house, the cellar just gave her the creeps. Jim said he'd fix it up so she'd never have to be afraid again. He even promised to cover over the crawl space with drywall.

She smiled at the thought of Jim. After she got that huge insurance settlement from the accident, she knew that things were finally going to be all right. She had always said that if it weren't for bad luck, she'd have no luck at all, but that money proved her wrong. Her luck was finally turning.

She glanced at Buddy and felt a twinge of guilt. That child was the cause of all her bad luck. His loser of a dad had knocked her up. Sure, they married, but he'd been abusive and when he finally left, he took what little money they had, as well as the TV, stereo, and the truck. He also left her to deal with unpaid back rent on their public housing apartment, and even worse, he left her with a ten-year-old boy labeled emotionally disturbed and neurologically impaired thanks to a few bad beatings when he'd been a toddler.

Then … then … the insurance settlement came and turned her life around. She was still smiling as she remembered purchasing this place. It had been a wreck, but like a knight on a white steed, Jim showed up on her door looking for work the day after she moved in.

"Mom, quit daydreaming and answer me, can we open it?"

Janet stopped smiling. "Why don't we wait for Jim to get home?" she said, and realized her mistake immediately.

"I don't need to wait for him," Buddy snapped. "I don't need his permission to do anything."

Janet opened her mouth to protest as Buddy grabbed the hammer Jim left out this morning and smashed the lock on the wooden box.

"NO," she screamed as the lock held but the wood around it splintered. She had no idea why she was breaking out in a cold sweat and panicking, but she felt a sick churning in the pit of her stomach as she stared at the box. She was suddenly terribly afraid of what was inside. She just knew it had to be something beyond awful. "Please stop!" she cried and grabbed at Buddy's hands, but he was faster and threw open the lid.

"Oh God," she moaned as the churning turned to pain. She thought that maybe she was having a heart attack as the breath froze in her throat. What horrors had her son impulsively unleashed she wondered as she doubled up in agony. She wanted to cry out and beg Buddy to slam the lid, but instead, she fell to the floor and the world drifted away out of her grasp.

Janet opened her eyes. She was confused. Why was she on the floor? Then she remembered. Buddy was sitting next to her. He was holding a black piece of silky, shiny cloth and he was crying.

"Buddy."

Buddy stopped sobbing. "Mom!" he shouted. "You're alive! I thought you were dead."

Janet managed a weak smile. She sat up and was surprised to discover that she felt fine. No weakness, no nausea. She reached over and patted her son's head. "I guess I fainted," she said, red with embarrassment. How typically and melodramatically weak to faint at a climactic moment. She remembered her terror, the fear that paralyzed her. "Buddy … honey, what was in the box?" she forced herself to ask.

"This!" Buddy exclaimed with total, childish excitement as he held up his hand.

Janet stared at a small black and white tuxedo partially covered with a shimmering black cape. After a second's hesitation she realized she was looking at a hand puppet. Her eyes focused on the wooden face and she smiled, it looked like a handsome classic movie star. It even had a tiny top hat.

She started to laugh. A puppet, an old fashioned child's toy. She'd fainted over a puppet!

Suddenly the laughter froze in her throat. Why was it in a locked box?

"Buddy, take that filthy thing off your hand, you don't know where it's been," she snapped.

Buddy looked down at the puppet and then up at his mother. "Ah, Mom, it's fine."

"Put it down!"

"No!" Buddy shouted back. "I'm keeping it and you can't stop me!"

Janet stopped yelling. She could tell by Buddy's tone that he was about to go over the edge and then he'd be out of control. *God, I hate Al for doing this to Buddy.* "Ok, honey, keep the puppet for now."

It didn't work. "For now! He's mine for always. I hate you, you bitch. I hate you. I love my puppet. He's the only friend I've got and you aren't going to take him away."

Janet watched with resignation as he headed for a full tantrum kicking the television stand and knocking over the end table. She didn't say a word as he ran from the house; she just hoped he wouldn't hurt any one's pet or property.

"It is all right and I love him," Janet reminded herself. "He's my son and I love him. Yes, I love him." She hated the fact that her litany was getting more and more difficult to repeat. She hated the fact that she was so tired of being on the losing end of life. She wondered why she always seemed to make the wrong choice, why she was always stuck with all the problems that others created. Why did she have to be the caregiver when all she really wanted was for someone to take care of her, to give her unconditional love.

She glanced out the window at the daffodils waving in the breeze and the trees just beginning to bud. She didn't see her son anywhere and hoped he wasn't cold.

Janet shrugged and muttered, "I'll throw that nasty thing out after he goes to sleep," she muttered and looked at the broken crate. She walked over to it and gasped. It was full of dolls, very, old, fragile dolls, and even to her untrained eye, she instinctively knew they were worth a small fortune.

When Jim came home that night, he looked at the dolls as she stood by. "What do you think?" she asked.

"I think that maybe they are worth something, just don't get your hopes up. I'll take them to a dealer tomorrow."

She nodded and made dinner. As she was cooking she felt a soft caress on the back of her neck. She smiled and turned around to kiss Jim. She jerked back as Buddy lowered his arm. The disgusting puppet was still on his hand.

"Hi Mom," Buddy said and rubbed the puppet tenderly across her cheek. "The puppet wanted to say 'Hi.' What's for dinner?"

Janet shuddered. "Don't touch me with that thing!" She immediately felt guilty. Buddy couldn't help the way he acted. She knew he needed more help then she could give him and she worried that he was eventually going to have to be locked away if his outbursts got worse and he became a menace to others. So far he'd only hurt himself, which was bad enough, but at least she'd been able to get him meds for that, when she could afford it. Maybe, if the dolls worked out, she could have enough to get better insurance. All she needed was a little more money and some good luck and she could get this house fixed up, and pay off all the debt Al had left her. The insurance settlement was a good start, but it wouldn't last forever.

Buddy didn't even blink, "Come on, Mom, the puppet is great. He says he likes you a whole lot. He says he loves you. So can I keep him? I really want to keep him."

She could tell by the tone of his voice that she better not argue. "I guess, if you really like that dirty, old thing that much, we can wash it."

"Thanks Mom!"

After Buddy went to bed that night, Janet went into his room to get the puppet. It was still on his hand and she had to struggle with it to get it off. She tugged, and finally it came off. She was surprised that it wasn't dirty at all, in fact it felt nice in her hand, still warm from Buddy.

In the laundry room, she studied the puppet and actually smiled. It was such a handsome face: dark eyes, smiling lips, a pencil thin mustache under a perfect nose. So handsome, and yet, the smile was just the smallest bit cruel, turning up slightly at the corners and the painted flat eyes looked, she groped for the word, looked . . . looked sort of sinister. She laughed at herself. "Too much imagination, Janet. Get a grip," she muttered, dropped it next to the washing machine and went up to her bedroom to watch TV with Jim.

The next morning when she went to wake Buddy, she saw the puppet back on his hand. She frowned. *The kid was definitely being difficult.* "Come on, Buddy, give me the puppet so I can clean it."

Buddy opened his eyes, "Morning Mom, I'll give it to you later, it wants to stay with me right now."

Janet sighed and left the room; she just didn't have the energy this morning. It was Saturday and Buddy played all day with the puppet on his hand. Every time Janet tried to get it, he insisted that the puppet didn't want to leave him.

When Jim came home, he held up five one hundred dollar bills. "Look what the dolls brought in!" he shouted and hugged her. "A windfall!"

She looked at the money and felt letdown. She had hoped the dolls were worth more, she had been sure of it, but once again her luck wasn't really good. Five hundred dollars was nice, but wasn't going to solve any of her problems.

Janet hugged him back, but she couldn't shake off that hollow feeling in her gut that things just weren't right.

After dinner, she went to bed early and woke with a start. Someone was in bed with her, touching her thighs, caressing them. It wasn't Jim, he'd gone out for a few drinks with the guys, and besides it wasn't his touch. He didn't know about gentle. She lay perfectly still and held her breath. The soft warm touch moved a little higher.

As the hand moved up even more, the paralysis left her and she sat up reaching for the light. "Who's there?" she screamed. She felt lightheaded, feared she'd faint again, as the room lit up and she saw her son on the bed next to her. The puppet was on his hand and he looked startled.

"Buddy!" she screamed. "Buddy, what are you doing!"

"Huh?" Buddy mumbled looking around the room. "What am I doing here? Why'd you wake me?"

Janet felt like throwing up. Buddy was sleep walking and acting out his fantasies. What was she going to do? Her little boy had almost molested her in his sleep.

She jumped out of the bed and took a few steps away from him. "Buddy, don't you ever, ever do that again!"

"Buddy looked confused and hurt. "Do what, Mom?"

She didn't know how to answer. "Don't . . . don't touch me."

"I didn't."

"Yes, you did!" she shrieked, starting to lose control. "Don't ever touch me again. Now get out of here and go back to bed."

Watching him get up, Janet felt the tears on her cheeks. He was only a little boy, her little boy, and she could tell by the look on his face that she had hurt him. Suddenly, she moved around the bed and hugged him. "I'm sorry, honey. Mommy loves you. I'm sorry. I just had a bad dream."

"I love you too, Mom," Buddy said and hugged her back. She felt the puppet gently rub her hair, a soft, lingering touch, and Buddy added, "And the puppet says he loves you, too."

Janet avoided being too close to Buddy the next morning. She was ashamed about the way she was acting, but she just didn't know what to do. He hadn't touched her again, but still, what was a mother to do when her young son makes sexual advances? She had no one to ask advice. It was times like this that she felt the loneliest, when she realized that no one really loved her the way she needed. No one was there to take care of her, to ask nothing of her at all,

After lunch, she told him to play outdoors since it was warm and sunny. She watched through the kitchen window, as he talked to the puppet. He was sitting on the dirt in the tiny fenced-in back yard, having a one-sided conversation. He was getting upset and his voice was growing louder and louder. Soon he was shouting. "I can't . . . I won't!"

She watched from the window, fascinated. Without warning, he slapped himself across the face with the puppet. Hard. She heard the smack through the glass. Then he smacked himself again. She started for the door as he picked up an empty flowerpot and cracked it over his head. She saw the blood and ran to him.

He sprawled the ground and cried.

"Why'd he do it, Mommy?" he wept as she wrapped a towel around his head. "I thought he was my friend. I thought he liked me. But he likes you better."

"Shhh," Janet crooned and started to rock him in her arms. She wondered what he was talking about. She was pretty sure she knew the answer, that her son was hearing voices in his head. He was insane!

She washed him up, took him on the bus over to the emergency room, explained that he had fallen while playing and let them bandage him up. After she got them home, she gave him a pain pill and put him to bed.

She'd have to talk to Jim later. In the meantime, she wanted that puppet gone. During the entire ordeal the thing never left Buddy's hand. He even insisted on bathing with it earlier that day. And now he was convinced that it was talking to him, telling him to hurt himself.

She tiptoed into Buddy's room and tried to remove the puppet. It didn't budge, She struggled, pulled, tugged and ripped at it, but Buddy's hand must have been balled into a death grip fist.

Wiping the sweat from her forehead, she stopped struggling and gave up. Jim would have to get it from him when he got back from wherever it was he went. Three hours later when Jim came in, she rushed to him. "Jim. Buddy got hurt today. I had to take him to the emergency room."

Jim frowned. "You did? How much did it cost?"

She ignored the question and the implications that he never asked how Buddy was or whether he was hurt badly. "I need you to help me get the puppet off his hand."

Jim's expression changed. "The puppet? What on earth are you talking about?"

She heard the desperate edge to her voice, "Don't ask me anything, just help me!"

Jim walked into Buddy's room, Janet right behind him. Buddy was out cold. Jim went over and grasped the puppet. He pulled, but only succeeded in jerking the boy to one side of the bed. "Tough," he grunted and gave it a yank.

The puppet . . . the hand . . . the arm suddenly lashed out. It grabbed at Jim's throat throwing him off balance. Buddy had Jim, a full-grown man, down on the floor. And he was trying to choke him. "Don't you ever touch it!" Buddy screamed. "Don't you ever bother it. Die! Die! Die!"

Jim rolled over and tried to pry the puppet-covered hand off him. Janet stared, not knowing what to do. She felt a like a deer caught in headlights. Mesmerized. She watched as his strong fingers worked the puppet's tiny arms, clawing at it. She gasped as she saw him punch Buddy full in the face.

The boy fell backwards, blood gushing from his nose and mouth.

"Stop it," she screamed and ran to her son. She was cradling him in her arms when she heard grunts behind her. She turned and saw the puppet was still attached to Jim's throat.

She gasped and started pulling at the puppet. Suddenly, it popped off and she fleetingly wondered what had held it in place since it was free of Buddy's hand.

She started crying. Buddy really needed help.

Jim got up cursing, and went to the phone. "That boy needs to be put away," he said in a raspy tone. He rubbed his reddened throat. "I'm calling an ambulance."

Janet spent the rest of that night and the next day and night at the hospital. She nodded dumbly as the doctors explained about mental illness and the treatments available. She realized that they were going to lock her baby up, but at least he'd finally get the help he needed.

Janet was numb by the time she got home. She went into Buddy's room to clean up the blood and get rid of that horrible puppet. To her surprise, it wasn't there. She shrugged and washed the stains off the floor. Struggling against exhaustion, she put up a load of laundry and went to find Jim. She figured he'd be asleep. The sun was just coming up when Janet stumbled into her bedroom. She stopped, the exhaustion forgotten.

Her eyes were riveted at the sight of Jim.

He was standing, his back pressed to the wall, his face distorted with terror. She saw the puppet. It was on Jim's right hand and gripped in both its tiny hands was a large, serrated, kitchen knife.

Janet watched in fascinated silence as the blood glinted off the shiny blade. She saw the blood stains on Jim's pant leg and T-shirt. He looked at her and their eyes met. He pushed the puppet with his free hand trying to keep it away from his body. She could see his muscles quivering as he struggled with himself. "Make it stop!" he screamed. "Get it off me!"

Janet jumped into action. She grabbed at the puppet-clad arm and pulled with all her might. The arm seemed to move away from Jim. She relaxed a little and before she could react, the puppet ripped from her hands and plunged the knife into Jim's stomach. She grabbed and pulled it back, then ripped the knife from its grasp as Jim's shrill scream echoed in her ears.

She threw the knife to the side and helped Jim slide to the floor. He held the wound with his free hand and said, "I'm . . . I'm sorry. The … mon … money is in the garage, I'm sorry … just get it off my hand and make it stop … "

His head bowed forward and Jill watched his ragged breathing to make sure he wasn't dead. The blood was leaking from his gut and he groaned. She took his hand and removed the puppet. She was still carrying it when she called the police and she was still carrying it when they loaded Jim onto the ambulance. She absently rubbed the smooth, satiny fabric against her face as the police officer repeated, "Lady, you are so lucky you stopped him. Jim Owens is wanted, killed three women in two states. There's even a reward posted for his apprehension. Consider yourself very, very lucky."

She nodded and showed them to the door. Let the police think what they liked, she decided. Let them think she'd done this to Jim in self-defense. She had too much to think about to be worried about the police.

After they left and the house was quiet, she went out to the tiny garage and found Jim's toolbox. There was a check for $85,000 from a rare, antiques collection house made out to cash. *That bastard*, she thought, finally beginning to feel emotion again. *This has to be the money from the dolls!*

Janet looked at her hand and was shocked to discover the puppet on it. A surge of fear began to work its way from the tip of her head down to her toes. About halfway down, the icy horror turned into a rush of warmth. "I love you," echoed in her head and she nodded, realizing that it did.

She went back into the house and climbed into her bed, exhaustion returning and slamming her like a physical force. She had known all along that the puppet was something evil, that it was more than a puppet. She knew it from the start.

"I have to get rid of it," she mumbled. But … she … was … just … too … tired. "I'll take care of it when I wake up."

She slept and dreamed, and when she woke, she was smiling. She was rich. Between the dolls and the reward, she was really, really rich.

And as the puppet on her hand lovingly caressed her breasts, her smile widened because she realized she was finally and unconditionally loved.

SUMMER

WEAVING TANGLED WEBS

August 15

This is very difficult. Dr. Allen feels that a journal will help. He said I suffer from stress. Can you imagine that, stress? If only Dr. Allen knew the truth, then he'd realize a journal could never be enough.

What the hell, I'm willing to give this a try. Maybe putting my life down on paper will get rid of some of this pent-up frustration.

This is almost fun. After I'm done I have to find a good hiding place so Troy never sees it. I certainly don't want him to know I went to Dr. Allen about my sprained wrist. He'd be furious if he found out I wasted some of the grocery money on myself.

Do I start writing about my life from day one? *I was born on the poor side of town to my mother.* No, too common.

How about, *I have lived my life as a statistic: child of an abusive alcoholic, married to an abusive alcoholic—*

Nah, this is silly, Dr. Allen said to write about my daily life, so here goes.

Today was kind of standard. Troy worked late, went out drinking and still isn't home so I know tonight will be all right. The brats are quiet, I think they're in bed or else maybe out robbing a bank. I don't care, just so everyone leaves me alone.

I guess summer's almost over because I found another spider in the laundry room. Ugly bastard! I wonder why they're so God-awful ugly. If there is anything I hate more than my life, it's those eight-legged nightmares.

I stood next to the dryer and watched it scurry across the top. At first I recoiled, edging away from the small black thing. If it had been any bigger, I would have been terrified, but it was tiny and I felt in a brave mood for a change. I thought about killing it, but didn't. I don't know why, but sometimes I feel sorry for the really little guys. I sometimes wonder if they feel as frightened of me as I do of my world.

I didn't kill it, but I gave it a stern warning. "Stay out of my way or you are going to be dead meat," I said and wondered, *could I get locked away for threatening an arachnid? Is there is a government agency to protect household infesters?* Sparing its insignificant life made me feel powerful, like I was in control for once.

August 16

Today life went from pathetic to intolerable. Troy woke up with a hangover (no big surprise there). He was exceptionally miserable and I tried to tiptoe around him until he left. Only it didn't work, he found my house-cleaning annoying.

I was on my knees washing up the spilled juice, cereal, and assorted unidentifiable foods off the floor when he walked into the kitchen. He poured himself a cup of coffee and obviously didn't notice me stooped over. Tripping over my feet, he stumbled and dumped most of his coffee on my back.

"Shit, woman!" he yelped, wiping at a few dark brown spots on his shirtsleeve. "You trying to kill me?"

Incapable of answering, I blinked tears away as fiery pain etched a red welting design on the skin across my shoulders. *I hate you,* I thought, rolling over to rub my burned skin in the cool soapy water puddled on the floor.

That was a mistake. I saw it coming, but didn't have time to roll away. He kicked me. That son of a bitch kicked me in the ribs while I was down. And for doing what? For cleaning up the filthy mess his rotten kids leave every morning before they go off to mug senior citizens or maybe actually attend a day of school when it was in session.

I tried to draw in a breath but couldn't. He had booted the air right out of me. For a moment, dark spots danced in front of my vision. I thought I was going to pass out but fought to draw in some air and stay alert.

Slowly, it seems to get slower with each assault, I worked my way up to my knees, then to my feet. As I stood there swaying, holding my bruised side, I tried to decide whether I should run away or kill him.

"Mandy!" he bellowed. "Just don't stand there like a useless piece of garbage. Fix me another coffee and iron a clean shirt. Fast!"

Decision made, I walked over to the coffee pot right next to the knife drawer. Slowly, ever so slowly, I poured him another cup and carried it over to him. It made me feel a little better to annoy him by moving in slow motion. Then I ironed his damned shirt.

Yes, I know I'm weak and the bastard needed to be punished, but it just wasn't in me. I don't think I am capable of hurting a bug.

Sometimes, I envy the female spider who can bite off the head of her mate without blinking an eye. Now there is a woman who doesn't get dumped on. I think I'd like to come back in my next life as a black widow. Yeah a widow sounds really good, especially a poisonous one.

Troy put on his shirt, came up close to me and raised his arm over his head. I cringed; ready for the blow I knew was coming.

POP! His shoulder cracked loudly in the silent room and he lowered his arm. "Ah, that's better. Well, guess I'll go now," he said, and bent over to give me a sloppy wet kiss. Then he went off to his little executive office at the bank.

I think I like writing everything down like this. It helps me channel my anger. I can hate the words instead of everything else around me.

August 16/17 (3 A.M.)

Well, here we go again. I couldn't sleep so I decided to finish writing about my day. I guess I'll pick up where I left off.

I finished cleaning the kitchen and started on the powder room. I was just about to scour the sink when I saw "it." Revulsion clutched my stomach, squeezing it, forcing my breakfast back up my throat. I whipped my hand away from the porcelain bowl terrified "it" would leap off the drain stopper and start ripping the flesh from my arms.

"It" sat there, still and silent. I felt like taking off my shoe and smashing its dime-sized black, furry body to a pulpy green and yellow mush. Could it possibly be the same one as yesterday? Although it looked like the same kind of spider, this one was bigger. Big enough to scare me. I watched it with distrust, waiting for it to make a move toward me.

Suddenly one thread-like hairy leg lifted then the other seven followed. As "it" scurried up the rear of the sink, I backed off, cowering. Then the truth hit me, "it" was afraid, too. To that disgusting awful spider, I was the monster, just like Troy was to me.

With a surge of understanding, I decided I could be generous to a fellow creature, even one as grotesque as this arachnid. "I warned one of you guys yesterday, but I'll give you one more chance," I said picking up a wad of tissues. "But this time I mean it. Get out of my house and stay out!"

I gingerly grabbed it with the tissues, holding it at arm length in case it attacked. I decided it was a she and added, "Go out and kill a mate or two for me." Then turning around, I heaved it out the open window giving the tissues a couple of good shakes.

I was brimming with compassion as I called, "There you go, little sister. Have another shot at life and make it better than mine."

Only I wasn't as gentle as I thought and one skinny twitching leg stuck to the tissues. So much for compassion.

When Troy came home he acted like nothing happened earlier. Once again we were a perfect family. Except, that when the doors were closed and the blinds drawn, the maid/whore/punching bag were all packaged in one convenient sack. That's what I feel like most of the time; a shapeless, useless, burlap sack laying by the side of the road waiting to be kicked or run over by an eighteen-wheeled semi.

As I tried to fall asleep, I recited my usual mental chant, another day concluded. That's how I spend my days, counting them off, waiting for the final victimization.

Sometimes I try to recall bright moments, but they were too few and too often snuffed out, just like Denny. Even from the beginning, Troy and this marriage were hollow and joyless. On our first date, Troy forced me to have sex with him. I had been a twenty-three-year-old virgin on a blind date. After that night, I was a victim of date rape. Mom helped a lot. She alternated between calling me a tramp and telling me how lucky I was that someone could like a plain, spineless, old maid enough to make it with her.

Even back then, I was already beaten, both mentally and physically. I was totally submissive to my existence. There was no fight in me, just acceptance of whatever fate handed out.

Troy knew when I didn't turn him in and actually agreed to go out on a second awful date, that he had found the perfect wife. Yes, the perfect wife: dull, mousy, scared of everything, I was that special someone to raise his kids. I'd cook for them, clean for them, and cover up for them whenever they'd go on one of their juvenile crime sprees.

We both knew what we were getting with each other, but marriage seemed a better alternative to spending the rest of my days caring for Mom. Fat, crippled by decades of alcohol abuse, she'd crippled me mentally. Beating me and browbeating me until I was too afraid to think for myself. The few times I did fight back, I paid dearly with broken bones and shattered spirit.

It seemed that I was doomed to wait on her forever and then came Troy. True, he was cruel and explosive, but his viciousness wasn't aimed at me like hers was. He didn't hate me personally. He hated life's blows and took them out on me.

I guess I've been writing a long time. My fingers and wrist ache and the sky is starting to get light. I think I'll quit and try to get some sleep.

August 17

I did fall back to sleep but had an awful nightmare. I dreamed I was wrapped in spider webs, caught in yet another trap. I spent the morning resting as soon as everyone left. In the afternoon, I went upstairs to clean some more. It seems that cleaning the house is the only thing that keeps me sane. I can scrub away all my bitterness and hurts for a while. I felt accomplishment in a clean home, it was something I'd never had growing up.

Mom, the drunken pig, never cleaned, never cooked, and never cared. She never cared about me or Denny. I don't even remember her crying at his funeral. Of course I don't remember much about that time. I had to be drugged because my constant sobbing interfered with her stricken mother routine. Denny—handsome, blond, big brother Denny—was the only person who ever really loved me and he died. Sent to the store for a bottle of booze, he never came home. She didn't care that she made him go out in a storm for her scotch. She didn't care that a car smashed him, smashed his bike. She never cared.

I cared and everything died with him.

So now I clean, every day, religiously. I scrub and scour looking for a ray of hope in the sparkling white enamel. I went into the twin's room, a nightmare of junk, crumbs, and wet sheets and started to strip the plastic-lined beds. Those two monsters were every stepmother's worst nightmare. No wonder their mother abandoned that family, two bad seeds and a rotten pod.

As I pulled the urine-stained sheet off of Ricky's bed, movement caught my eye. There was another spider, black and velvety, sitting on a corner of the mattress. This one had to be the big brother of the one from yesterday, at least the size of a half dollar.

Dropping the sheet, I slowly backed out of the room and closed the door. I ran downstairs and grabbed the bug spray then dashed back. Gingerly opening the door, I found the bed empty. Giving a spritz just to be on the safe side, I slammed the door and let the sheets dry on the floor. I wasn't going back in there. I was afraid it was the same spider, feasting and growing on the hate in this place. Maybe growing on the hatred it must feel for me since I crippled it.

It seems that I am becoming obsessed with spiders. This is silly, but I wonder if it is coincidence that the spiders keep getting bigger or does this house generate enough negative energy to cause a monster to grow. I'm afraid, more afraid than usual. What if that spider really is growing? What if, what if, what if? I don't have any answers and I guess I never will.

August 20

Thursday, two days ago, had to be the absolute worst day of my life. It was the day that all my nightmares came true all at once. I can't believe I'm still sane and functioning, but maybe I'm not. Maybe this is the ramblings of a madwoman. I don't know anymore. Am I free or am I being hunted. Who knows?

Thursday she "it" appeared next to the washing machine in the laundry room. Oh, I know now that it's her and she's going to get me. She got big, a real growing girl. About the size of a saucer, I found her on a strand of silk hanging right over the washer, bouncing in front of my face at eye level. I turned to run and bumped into Troy who came home early from a late liquid lunch.

I screamed, not sure what to be more frightened of, which was the more monstrous. Troy snarled and shoved me against the washer. I felt the metal and knew I would have a few more bruises before he finished. "God, you're an ugly thing," he muttered, his breath stinging my nose. "Why'd I ever marry something as pathetic as you?"

I knew what was coming, he loved angry sex. It was the only way he could get hard. The more he hurt me, the harder he'd get. "You're not even fit to take care of Ricky and Nicky. Why, you're not fit to live!"

He grabbed my neck and suddenly I knew he was really going to kill me. All the other times were just practice, this was the real thing.

"Stop!" I squeaked, unable to fight off my own death. "Stop, that hurts!"

His grip tightened, I could feel his fingers digging into my flesh. The bones in my neck were grinding together and it was only a matter of seconds before the vertebrate crumbled to splintered dust. As the pain and pressure increased on my collapsing windpipe, I feebly tried to slap his hands off. I needed to breathe.

I was dying, and the worst, the most degrading thing about it was he was getting off. The tighter he choked me, the harder he was grinding against me. He was breathing heavy, a track of spit running from the corner of his mouth down into the stubble on his chin. And he was smiling, panting, coming. My God, he was coming!

That was worse than anything, worse than death! The bastard was not only murdering me, he was depriving me of every last dignity.

I wasn't going to die that way! I refused. For the first time in my poor excuse of an existence, I fought for me. I grabbed at his hands trying to pull them away but couldn't. I slapped at his face but things were blurring, growing darker. It was ending and I knew I had lost.

My last thoughts were that I had finally fought back. Some solace, huh? Then out of the blue, that spider fell from above onto my face. It scurried onto his hands and it was really odd but just as consciousness faded, I noted that it only had seven legs and an oozing stump.

I wasn't quite out completely. Suddenly, I heard Troy bellow like a wounded animal and I felt myself slide down as the pressure disappeared. Sitting on the floor, propped against the washer, I gratefully gasped air, amazed to be alive. My vision slowly returned, and I was alone. Troy was gone; all I could see was a trail of blood droplets leading away from the laundry room. "I hope it's his," I rasped as I rubbed my agonized throat.

I remembered that spider, the one with seven legs. If it were the same one, growing bigger every day, it was going to get me. I had ripped off its leg. It may have been during an act of kindness, but I maimed it. It was going to get me.

Pushing myself up, I staggered out of there as fast as I could. I had to escape. I had to get away from that madman and the spider. I really did want to live. I really did. If I survived, I swore I would get help. I'd learn to love me. Even if no one else in this entire world could find in their hearts a place for me, I'd love me.

I'd spent my whole life wanting love, searching for it, settling for anything, any tidbit of affection. This whole situation was my fault. I stayed with Troy even though I knew he was horrible and cruel. I knew he only wanted a slave for those kids, those nasty, hateful kids. All these years and all I had to do was walk out that door. Well, I would now. I was going.

Only, he grabbed me from behind as I reached for my pocketbook in the living room. He spun me around and I saw his hand was wrapped in a blood soaked handkerchief and there was a bleeding red welt on his cheek. "Where do you think you're going?" He snarled as he wiped at his face with his shirtsleeve. "Look at me! This is your fault! That spider bit me. It's all your fault! Filthy house, I always said you were useless!"

He was insane, I could see it in his eyes and he was still going to kill me. As he raised his hand to slap me, I nailed him, kicked him where it did some good. I was done being battered. If one of us was going to die, it wasn't going to be me.

I grabbed my pocketbook and ran for the door. I would have made it if those kids hadn't jumped out of nowhere and tripped me.

"We hate you!" They both shrieked and started kicking me.

I remembered the times they burned my clothes, cut me with a knife, killed our neighbors' pets, set the school on fire, and kicked and hit smaller kids.

I jumped up and punched them. First Nicky, then Ricky. I really wanted to let them have it, but it was too late. Troy was on his feet and coming for me. I looked around desperately, saw my only escape was back to the laundry room. I ran for it. I was more willing to face that spider then them.

I slammed the door, locked it, and moved the dryer in front of it. I was never a strong woman, but believe me when I say I found the strength to move that machine. I huddled in the corner of the room holding the bleach bottle as a weapon. They pounded and yelled, but for the moment I was safe. I saw movement and looked up. The spider, now the size of a dinner plate had flattened its body the way bugs can and was squeezing out of the room under the door that led to the garage.

Now, I was really safe, at least for the moment, that monster was gone and the other monsters had given up trying to break down the door. The garage entry was bolted from the inside so I could relax for the moment. I heard Troy yelling, "Forget it for now boys, she'll have to come out sometime. Then we'll take care of her."

Can you imagine how sick a family they must be to have a forty-year-old father plot to kill his wife with his two thirteen-year-old sons?

I fell asleep, my body and mind exhausted. When I woke the room was dark, darker than I remember any place being. Suddenly, I needed to get out. Get away from the dark, the spider and the madman. Slowly, I moved the heavy dryer, so heavy I don't know how I got it there. I made a space big enough to open the door. I listened at it, not breathing to hear better. Silence. Finally, with the bleach bottle opened and aimed, I went out to find the house dark and quiet. Too quiet. I instinctively knew I was alone.

I crept out the back door and stopped. A funny odor tickled my senses, strong and dangerous. Gasoline! I silently walked toward the front, hugging the wall. Turning the corner by the garage I tripped over two large white rocks, soft and sticky rocks!

I had to know what they were and why the fire that was to kill me had never been lit.

Gathering all my courage, I purposely tripped the movement sensitive floodlights by the garage door.

Horrible!

I doubled up and gagged. I may have hated them but I never wished a fate like this on anybody. Nicky and Ricky, wide-eyed and dead, were bound from the neck down in cocoons of spider silk. There was blood on the ground, but it looked like there was very little left in them.

They were going to torch me, yet I started to cry for them. I say started because something large and furry and velvet black was blocking the garage door. She was now the size of a medium sized dog. Yes, now I'm sure she thrived on hate. Twisting her head in my direction, it took a hesitant step toward me, than another.

It seemed like there was going to be no end to this nightmare!

As she closed in on me, I saw Troy inside the garage behind the monster. He had his hunting rifle. Wildly, he swung the barrel, pointing it first at me then at that mutant spider. He was so disturbed he couldn't decide who to kill first.

He started to laugh, a high hysterical giggle. "This is all your fault, bitch!" he mumbled between bursts of laughter.

Without thinking, I ducked down and picked up the cigarette lighter on the ground next to Nicky. I hadn't even realized that I'd noticed it. I flicked it on and threw it.

POOF!! That house went up like a piece of old newspaper. Troy, too. I heard his screams as I ran. I had the grocery money and our automatic bankcard in my pocketbook so I was set for a while.

Now here I am, a hunted woman in a cheap motel right off the interstate outside of town. To think that a week ago I was just an unhappy housewife who only dreamed of running away.

That was two nights ago and my nerves are frazzled. I hate the cornfield outside my back window. I keep imagining that the spider survived the fire and is out there waiting, hiding, in the tall green cornstalks. I know she'll find me because once a victim, always a victim.

I hear a crash in the bathroom. The window! Oh God, the bathroom door is opening . . .

August 21

I thought I'd written my last, last night. I thought I was really a goner when that door opened. I dropped my pen and jumped off the bed where I had been writing when I saw a long thin black hairy leg reach out. I wanted to run, only I couldn't, fear has locked my feet to the floor. In a wave of weakness my knees buckled and I fell backwards onto the bed. I lay there and waited for the end, praying it would be painless.

Filled with a deep sadness, filled with regrets, I closed my eyes and waited, and waited some more. Finally I opened them and saw her, now the size of a very large dog, standing beside me. I quickly squeezed my eyes shut, held my breath and went rigid with dread.

Instead of eating me, she just stood there and nudged me with her good front leg. And she whimpered. I opened my eyes, let out my breath and sat up. I forgot to be afraid. This wasn't in the script; victims and losers never get a second chance.

She nuzzled me, rubbing against me and I couldn't believe it but I swear she was doing the spider equivalent of purring! I gingerly reached out and touch her soft downy back. I don't know what I expected, but it felt nice like a cat. She responded by shivering, then rubbed me harder.

What do you know, somebody finally loves me. I guess kindness does pay off. I only have to wonder, did she grow from the hateful vibrations that filled our home or did she grow from my need. Could my sparing her life make her respond physically to my desperate situation? I think she too felt that brief moment of empathy and came to my aid.

I'll never know, but in the meantime I think it's time to end this journal for a while and start finding my new life. So until I settle into my niche, I think I'll take my new friend and move in with Mom. I know she won't care. She won't dare!

BUCKETS OF FUN

Becca was coming home from camp!

Gloria glanced out the window at the glorious morning and smiled. She'd been upset for days, but now she was excited. She still felt hurt by her daughter's childish outburst last week. She remembered how Becca had been at the edge of the lake, tears streaming down her cheeks as she hugged her yellow bucket and beach ball. The seven-year-old girl had sobbed, "I hate Mommy. She's making me go away. I hate her so much, I wish she was dead!"

Those words felt like a physical blow to the gut. Gloria had blinked back shocked tears, then strode over to her daughter. "Come on, Becca."

"Don't want to go. I wanna stay and play."

"I know, Honey, but there are no children here. Don't you want to have friends to play with?"

"My toys are my friends! They love me!"

"Really!" Gloria snapped, still smarting from the childish hate-filled wish.

"Yes, they told me so!"

Gloria didn't bother to argue about talking beach toys. She grabbed Becca by the arm, dragged her to the car and drove her to overnight camp.

The week had gone by so fast and yet so slow. But today, Jack was picking Becca up after work. They'd be home for dinner. Gloria stared at the beach, so calm and quiet in the morning sunshine. The water sparkled and the sand was smooth except where the bucket and shovels were strewn about.

She walked down to the toys and frowned. *Why were they out again,* she wondered, positive no one with kids was visiting this side of the lake.

Probably teenagers! Yep, teenagers making a mess. She strode past the toys to stand knee deep in the perpetually cold water and wondered why the water never grew warm, even on hot, sunny days like this. It didn't really matter to her, she never went above her knees. That was as deep as she ever went. People asked her why they lived there if she couldn't, wouldn't, swim or go out on a boat. "Because," she'd say, "Jack and Becca love it, and I enjoy painting the view."

Gloria decided to wade along the water's edge and then go back and pick up the beach toys. The icy bite of the water felt good contrasting with the warmth of the day. Ten feet down the beach, her foot went down into a huge hole that hadn't been there yesterday and she plunged forward, falling face down in the shallow water. Her head went under and hit the sand. She panicked, splashing and screaming, inhaling the lake. Water rushed down her throat and she choked on the burning sandy liquid until she instinctively pushed herself up. Kneeling in the shallow water, her throat on fire, pain making her eyes tear, she wondered with a deep sense of dread, *Who. . . why would someone dig such a deep hole?*

Her brain spun with residual terror and her face burned red with embarrassment over panicking in such shallow water. She took stock: her throat hurt, her face hurt, and her ankle hurt. "Great start to a beautiful day," she croaked and wiped a trickle of bloody water off her nose.

Limping slowly, painfully toward the cottage she wondered why the toys kept appearing on the beach. Twice she had almost fallen into large holes dug next to the patio, exactly where she usually set up her easel and oil paints. "I should call the police," she muttered and bent to gather up the bucket. The slight morning breeze kicked up, blowing sand onto her wet clothes and hair. Movement on the edge of her vision made her turn and look at the lake. "Now how'd that get out of the shed?" she muttered as she watched Becca's favorite beach ball drifting on the tiny ripples, the growing wind taking it out toward the middle.

"Damn it," she grumbled, realizing she would have to go and get it. Becca would carry on if her ball was gone Gloria really wanted this perfectly beautiful day to be a happy reunion.

She hobbled to the shed and pulled out the small, child-sized inflatable boat and paddle. She looked for the vest, but couldn't find it. She stood, frozen with indecision. The few times she'd been on a boat, she never went out without a vest. Inspiration hit and she grabbed the inner tube and struggling, got it over her shoulders and around her waist.

Tugging the boat to the water, she was annoyed at how nervous she felt about going out alone. She forced her legs to bend, forced her heart to slow down to a less death defying rhythm, then she got in the boat and paddled. The sun felt warm on her hair and face, but the growing breeze was cooling her as she pushed the oar through the water.

The drifting ball bobbed just out of reach. Frustrated and a little scared of the chilled, dark water, Gloria pushed the paddle hard and grabbed out for the ball. Her fingertips brushed it away. She stretched farther.

The boat wobbled, tipped, and flipped. A cold wet wave of terror washed over her and she screamed as she fell. Then Gloria calmed down when she realized the inner tube was keeping her afloat. She squinted through the sun glare on the ripples and watched the inflatable boat speed away, chasing after the ball in the gusting wind.

"All right," she said, trying to remain calm and rational. "I'll doggie paddle back to shore," but the tube seemed to be fighting her, carrying her out deeper, almost, she thought, as if it had a mind of its own.

She clung to it, fighting to push herself to shore until she felt the tube around her waist getting soft. She flailed her arms and legs struggling to get it off and somehow succeeded.

Her head dunked below the water but she managed to hold onto the deflating tube. She bobbed up and saw the plastic plug that sealed the air hole had somehow popped opened. Struggling to stay afloat, she managed to blow it up, then clung to it, calling for help until she was hoarse. Hopefully someone would walk on the beach or go boating and hear her.

She could handle this, she decided, calming down. She might even drift to the other shore. Even if no one came by, Jack and Becca would be home by nightfall and find her.

All she had to do was keep her grip on the ring and stay afloat. Then she saw the plug pop out again and heard the hissing air. She blew it up a second time, pushed in the plastic sealer hard and waited.

The sun beat down but its warmth couldn't penetrate the icy current below the surface.

"All I need to do is hold on and wait," she said through chattering teeth and watched in disbelief as the plug suddenly seemed to wiggled clear of the sealed hole. She weakly blew, slowly inflating the ring and then struggled with numb fingers to push the little plug back in. The cold water was drawing the feeling from her arms and the energy from her body.

"All I have to do is wait for help. Just gotta hold on," she assured herself over and over as the lethargy that comes with hypothermia sapped her stamina and her will.

She clung to that inflatable ring, so weak and cold she didn't even have the strength to react when the air plug popped open . . . again.

A Friend of the Family

Dennis drove slowly, squinting through the pollen-filled sun glare. He scowled as Ronny blithered on about summer in the Jersey Pine Barrens and his old girlfriend, Starlynne. Ron was the bore of the fraternity and Dennis really hated when he started on his endless, droning stories.

In fact, he really hated Ron. That guy was a stinking do-gooder, a study and get good grades kind of creep. He wouldn't have even had to put up with Ron at all if his damned parents had paid the plane fare home. But no, they insisted he fend for himself, find a summer job, be a man. Thank God Ronny had invited him to their family cabin near the shore for the whole summer.

Dennis gritted his teeth and swatted at the horse-flies that were competing with the mosquitoes for his blood. The dirt road under his tires churned out a cloud of dust and he felt a tickle deep in his throat. Finally, they reached a rustic log cabin surrounded by an apparently unending forest of scrub pine trees.

He unfolded his long legs from the beat-up car he'd bought with the book and supply expense money his parents had sent him during the school year. He stretched and asked, "How far to the beach?"

Ronny sniffed the pine scented air like a puppy and answered, "The river is about a mile to the west, the back bay is about three miles southeast and the ocean's about fifteen miles due east. Atlantic City's about twenty miles from here. We're deep in the pines, real close to the home of Mother Leeds and her thirteenth child."

Dennis knew what was expected of him and decided to be polite. "Who?"

"Mother Leeds and her mystery child, kid number thirteen," Ronny answered, his voice deepening. "The Jersey Devil! The story goes that she had her last child on a stormy autumn night and as soon as he popped out, he spread bat wings and flew up the chimney."

"Really?" Dennis asked, feigning interest.

"Yeah, really! That was a couple of hundred years ago, but he still lives around here. Starlynne says she's seen him lots of times."

"I'll have to meet this Starlynne, she seems like a fascinating girl."

"Oh, she is," Ronny gushed, leading the way to the cabin. "She is!"

He unlocked the heavy door and Dennis looked around at the glistening spider webs covering the wooden furniture and shuddered. What had he gotten himself into? "Parents don't get up here much, do they?"

"Actually they were here last week. The bugs and plants take over as soon as you turn your back. Only the real Pineys like Starlynne seem to have a rapport with them. She's a pine witch."

Dennis was getting tired of hearing about this stupid girl who was probably ugly to boot. An illiterate, red-necked, hillbilly. A Piney. He'd never even heard the term till he crossed half the country to attend the University of Pennsylvania. Now, after spending two summers across the Delaware River at the Jersey Shore, he'd heard his fill of rural pine stories. There was the Jersey Devil to have to contend with, as well as mad murderers in the woods and sharks in the waters. *Didn't these people have anything better to do than make up stories to scare the shit out of each other?*

"So Ronny," Dennis said steering the conversation away from local lore. "What shall we do first, hit the beach or the casinos?"

Dennis loved the Jersey Shore. It was the land of opportunity. He knew that a good-looking guy like himself, tall and blond was everything rich beach chicks looked for. He could be set for life if he got the chance. Had to be thousands of lonely women just waiting for the opportunity to help make his life perfect.

"Neither," Ronny said interrupting his thoughts. "I thought we'd just go for a hike, maybe see some deer and if we're lucky, a couple of locals."

Dennis couldn't believe it; the stupid ass-wipe wanted to waste time on a 4-H nature walk. Better to go along with him for a while, he decided. After all, they had a whole month before Ronny's parents planned to use the cabin. Dennis figured if he played his cards right, he'd get by all summer vacation without having to get a job. He felt sure that he'd find some stupid broad to take him in for the other half of the summer, feeding him steak and caviar and buying him presents. Why, if he got real lucky, he could be out of this rural, bug-infested hell before the month was up.

He put on long jeans and sprayed himself with insect repellent. "Want some?" he asked, offering Ronny the can as he eyed the guy's white arms and the pale, skinny legs sticking out of his shorts.

"No thanks," Ronny answered. "Starlynne taught me a little on how to get along with nature. The bugs and I have a sort of pact."

Dennis rolled his eyes, this guy was just too much. "Okay, it's your blood."

The hike was beyond boring. Just as Dennis expected, Ronny pointed out flora and fauna, as if anyone really cared about the stinking bunnies and squirrels. He talked on as Dennis swatted at mosquitoes that didn't seem to notice the maximum-strength repellent he was wearing.

Just as he was about to give up all hope that something interesting was going to happen, Ronny stopped short and yelled, "Hey, Starlynne! Over here!"

Dennis looked around and saw her. He sucked in air through clenched teeth, then whistled low. He stared at a vision walking across a field of weeds, only the weeds seemed to bloom in front of her as she approached. He knew that was silly and figured the breeze must be pushing the hidden wildflowers up. Yet, the lavender and white flowers enhanced her glimmering beauty. She was white, pale like the snowy, bell-shaped buds that opened at her feet. Long golden-white hair hung past her shoulders.

He found himself crossing the field to meet her, although he didn't remember starting to walk. She smiled, color rushing to her cheeks as she walked right past him, holding out her hands to Ronny. Dennis stood amazed. The guy who couldn't get a date if his life depended on it, was hugging the most beautiful girl in the world.

Finally Ronny broke their spell. "Starlynne, I'd like you to meet Dennis."

Starlynne looked at Dennis and he noticed, with fascination, that her eyes, which at first appeared colorless, proved to be pale, early dawn blue. He grasped her partially extended hand and was surprised to feel her pull away. As he stared at her perfect features, all the color drained from her face, turning it chalk white. Her eyes widened and the pupils rolled up. She collapsed, folding slowly to the long grass.

"Holy Shit!" Dennis said, stunned.

Ronny knelt down and cradled her head in his lap. "Star, Star," he whimpered, pushing back her hair as if she were a child in need of comforting.

Slowly the color returned to her waxy face and her eyes fluttered open. "Bad...so very, very bad," she whispered and started to cry.

"What's bad, Star? What's the matter?" Ronny asked hugging her.

"N...n...nothing, it's all right," Starlynne said, getting up on shaky legs. "I'm fine now." She turned to Dennis and added, "I'm pleased to meet you." But she didn't extend her hand and she didn't smile.

Time seemed to stand still in the woods. By Saturday, Dennis was almost foaming at the mouth. He'd spent hours tearing the legs off spiders and the wings off dragonflies just to keep busy. He even welcomed an evening of miniature golf with Ronny and Starlynne at a tourist trap on Route 9. Starlynne, though she didn't actually ignore Dennis, seemed to avoid eye contact most of the evening. Occasionally he'd catch her sneaking a glance, but she'd quickly look away.

He finally got her full attention when they returned to his car. He dug through the trunk for one of the gifts he had picked up a few months back at an after Christmas sale. With a dramatic bow, he held out the gift-wrapped box to her.

Starlynne's cheeks flushed pink as she took the offered present. "For me?"

Dennis was constantly amazed by her sincere veneer. All girls expected gifts. He knew all about buying their lust. That's why he always kept a few gift-wrapped trinkets in the trunk, because, he knew that if he gave women enough trinkets, they all became whores and spread their legs.

He wanted Starlynne, at least for a few times. She really turned him on, just a glance from her made him hard. He wanted to feel her flesh next to his, he wanted to feel their sweat mingle. He wanted to taste her, relish her, have her. Then move on. After all, life wasn't rent-free and he'd need a babe to put him up by August and not in these stinking woods. The beach was calling him, but in the meantime, he'd buy Starlynne.

He watched her open the gift. He smiled as her eyes grew round and she cooed at the cheap silver-plated candleholders. She smiled at him, the first real heart-felt smile he'd gotten from her since they met. "Oh, Dennis, they're lovely! Are they really for me?"

"Of course they are, Starlynne. Anybody who is such a good friend to my buddy, Ron, should have anything she wants."

"Oh thank you!" she said as she took Ronny's hand. Dennis stared at her like she'd slapped him. How could she take his gift then go to the jerk?

He smiled and shook his head. The bitch was playing hard to get!

The next day they went canoeing on the Wading River. The water was warm and shallow and smelled of summer. Dennis would have been bored on the tiny boat, except that Starlynne had his full attention.

He liked the way her breasts pushed up against the white fabric of her blouse as she helped Ronny paddle the watercraft. He wondered how she would feel beneath his fingers, his lips. He closed his eyes and could almost feel them making love. He could hear her moaning with pleasure and wanted to join in when he suddenly remembered that they were in a canoe.

He opened his eyes to see why she was moaning. Ronny had his arm tangled in a thorn branch. He was dripping ruby rivers over his fingers and hers as they grasped the wound.

"Dennis, Help paddle. Please!" Starlynne pleaded.

Dennis pried the oar from Ron's bloody fingers. This ought to help improve my image with her, he thought as he used the oar and pushed off too hard. The small canoe tipped and everyone splashed into the murky water. He was surprised to discover the bottom thick with muck covering the remains of long dead trees and he wished he hadn't taken off his shoes.

With difficulty, he painfully waded to shore, trying not to catch his feet on the sharp stumps. He turned to see if Starlynne needed help. If he was lucky, maybe the idiot with her would drown. In fact, that was an excellent thought. If Ronny drowned, Starlynne would definitely turn to him, Ronny's best friend, for comfort.

Luck wasn't with him and the other two had also staggered to shore. Ronny was shaking, his teeth chattering, and his head lolling back. He was barely conscious. Starlynne shooed Dennis away. "I'll take care of this," she said and covered the gash with both her hands and moaned deep in her throat. Dennis watched as the blood flowing between her white-knuckled fingers slowly stopped. He figured she was being a human tourniquet but when she removed her hands from the wound a few minutes later, the bleeding had completely ceased. She stood up, swaying, and staggered to the water's edge.

Dipping her skirt in the river, Starlynne wiped the blood from her hands then went to Ronny and started washing him off.

"Hey, do you think that's a good idea, wetting that wound?" Dennis questioned. "He'll start bleeding again."

"No, he won't," she said.

When the arm was clean, Dennis stared in disbelief. The wound was gone. He could see a red line where the jagged cut had been, but even as he watched, it faded.

Ronny groaned, rolled over to his knees and threw up. "I'm sorry," he mumbled weakly. "I can't handle blood."

"Shhh," Starlynne said, "It's all right now."

Ronny smiled at her and Dennis was positive that if they had been alone they would both have left their virginity right there on the island.

Suddenly, Ron looked at Dennis and frowned. "Den, you're hurt, too! Starlynne, look, Dennis' foot is bleeding."

Dennis looked down and saw that he had sliced his foot. Suddenly aware of the stinging pain, he sank to the ground.

Starlynne seemed to be having a non-vocal conversation with Ronny. Finally, she nodded.

Ronny smiled. "It will be okay," he said to her.

Starlynne got up and walked over to Dennis. She placed her hands on his foot and shuddered violently. He could feel her vibrating and wondered if being a healer hurt. As if in answer, she screamed and let go. "I'm sorry, I can't!" she sobbed. "I can't help you. Bad, so very, very bad!" Turning away, she ran to the edge of the water.

"What does she mean by that?" Dennis demanded, angry that she'd used up all of her curative powers on Ronny.

"She's just drained, that's all," Ronny said standing up and offering a hand to Dennis.

"That's another thing," Dennis said, grasping Ronny's hand and pulling himself up. "She just about dies every time she has to touch me. You'd think the girl hated me or something."

"Nah," Ron said in a low voice. "She's just scared of you. She's a real innocent, not worldly like us. People scare her."

Dennis understood, she was scared all right. Scared of the feelings she felt when she was around a real man. Well, he just had to remember to go slow.

The guys righted the boat and the three of them paddled home in silence. Ron took Starlynne to her place and Dennis stayed at the cabin cleaning out his foot. The cut was superficial and had already stopped seeping.

When Ronny returned, he told Dennis about the tragedy surrounding Starlynne's family. "Her parents are dead," he explained in a hushed voice. "Bunch of rednecks got drunk on a windy, autumn night three years ago and went hunting for the Jersey Devil. Rumors always had it that her family housed the beast. Took it in whenever it got lonely. Anyway, the damn Pineys burned them up. Set their house on fire with all of them sleeping inside. Starlynne was the only one to survive the fire. And you know what else, all those crazy murderous bastards, well all of them disappeared."

Dennis snorted. "What do you mean, disappeared?"

"They all went out hunting or fishing at different times and none of them ever came back. The thirteenth Leeds child takes care of its friends."

"That's absurd!" Dennis said laughing. "You don't really believe that crap?"

"As a matter of fact, I do. Starlynne told me how she escaped. It helped her, but she still scares easily. She swears she is going to die young. She's told me over and over again she's going to die a horrible, violent death and nobody, not even 'it', will be able to save her." Ron shuddered. "I hope she's wrong, I pray it, because I'm going to marry my bog witch. I plan to be with her forever!"

"Well, enough of the pine lure for me," Dennis said getting up. "I'm going out to grab some sandwiches." He got in his car and started to pull out onto the main dirt road, but turned into Starlynne's driveway instead. Walking up the steps, he noted the wooden house was relatively new. He knocked and felt annoyed when she answered with a gasp. "You!"

"Yeah, me! Want to tell me why you hate me so?"

She hesitated.

"I'm alone," Dennis said pushing past her. "Now look, I'm not some bad guy who'd hurt you or anything. So why do you pretend to dislike me?"

"You are bad," Starlynne whispered. "You are so bad that you are going to be my death. I felt it in your touch."

He laughed. "Bad? Hey look, baby, I'm just a regular guy. I've never hurt anyone, so you can be damned sure I'm not going to kill you."

She shook her head, "You are a bad person, leave me and leave Ronny. He can't see you for what you are."

He stepped closer and grabbed her arms. "Look Starlynne, let's drop all this witch crap. I don't know how you healed Ronny but I have a pain I'd like you to heal for me."

Still gripping her arms, he forced her head back and kissed her. She didn't respond like women usually did so he kissed her harder, jamming his tongue deep into her mouth. She tried to pull away but he bore down on her harder, grinding against her. As he let go of one shoulder and groped at her breast she broke free and ran into the kitchen.

He followed her and grabbed her again. Forcing her down onto the table, he unzipped his jeans and managed to rip her panties off. He used his muscular legs to pry her thighs apart. He jammed into her, hard, surprised at how tight she felt. He heard her gasp with pain and jammed into her again and again, knowing that soon she'd come around and gasp with pleasure. Ignoring her sobs and struggles, grunting with his own effort, he fucked her until he was spent.

Sated, he pulled out. He was satisfied and as he stood up, he glanced down at Starlynne's face. He stared at her in surprise. Usually when he met the eyes of a lover, he saw gratitude, satisfaction, pleasure. He always made the chicks happy, but Starlynne was sobbing, making no sound, her chest heaving and tears streaming from the corners of her eyes.

"Hey what's the matter with you?" he asked. "Oh, I get it, the first time is always hard, but look Honey, you were fine, just fine. With a little practice you'll be great."

"Get out!" Starlynne yelled as she sat up. "You ruined me, now, get out!"

Dennis looked surprised, "Hey, what do you mean, ruined you? You can't tell me you didn't want it. Hell, Starlynne, everybody wants it."

She stared at him wide-eyed, then jumped off the table. "You think I wanted to be raped?" she hissed, reaching into a drawer and pulling out a long, sharp, serrated knife. "Get out before I kill you!"

"Rape?" Dennis was shocked. "You think I raped you? Hell, Honey, you are nuts. I don't take anything that isn't offered. You've been giving me those sideways looks. I know when a woman wants me!"

Starlynne let out a blood-curdling scream and lunged at him with the knife.

Dennis grabbed her wrists and squeezed. As her grip loosened on the weapon, he took it from her. "Look Starlynne, I'm not into this kind of thing."

He grinned at the girl in front of him and wagged the knife like an admonishing finger. "If you're a good girl, I won't tell Ronny you like it rough."

Starlynne charged again, baring her nails, going for his eyes. Without thinking, he shoved her away, forgetting about the knife in his hand. He stared at her as she stumbled back, as she stared down at herself, at the spreading stain of red on her chest.

He'd accidentally stabbed her!

He looked at the knife still in his hand, covered with her blood then back to her. Between her onrush and his shove, he'd stabbed her in the chest. *No, wait, he thought quickly, she had stabbed herself, yeah, she'd done all this to herself! She had rushed onto the glistening blade. I didn't do a damned thing wrong!*

She stood there in front of him, swaying, "Help... me," she whispered as she folded to her knees. She tried to stop the bleeding, clutching at her chest, but the blood continued to spread. "Help me, I...I can't stop it.... you ruined me. The..the rape..."

He thought about helping. He was trying to decide what to do, how to explain this to the authorities, but her words froze him. She was still trying to accuse him of rape! He watched her as she sank lower and fell over on her side. He stood there doing nothing as the word rape echoed in his head. He watched as she lay on the wooden floor in a spreading pool of blood. He stood above her, mesmerized, as her chest heaved up and down with each breath she struggled to take.

This can't be happening, he thought, *not to me!* "

Dennis started pacing back and forth wondering what he was going to do. He knew it was a sick accident, but he was a stranger here. How was he going to explain this when she was trying to ruin his life?

"This was supposed to be a vacation," he mumbled. "God, I'm supposed to go to law school after next year."

He had to get rid of her! Yeah, deep in the woods. With a history like hers, a mysterious disappearance would only add to the folklore. All he had to do was get rid of her.

Steeling his nerves, he scooped up his bloody burden and carried her into the woods. Deep into the forest, he dropped her in a small clearing. She was still breathing, still watching him. "Please!" she gasped. Don't leave me!"

He turned and ran all the way back to her place and washed up the blood. There was so much and it took a long time.

Afterward, he hid the knife in his car, grabbed a shovel and ran back into the woods. She was still breathing, still conscious, but so weak she couldn't move or speak. He wanted to say something explain to her that he had to do this, had to protect himself, but couldn't find the words. Instead he dug a hole and buried her. After all, he was sure she was dying anyway. It was dark and he worked under the light of the almost full moon. Suddenly, he realized he was being watched. He could feel the eyes on him. He finished filling the hole, threw down the shovel and rushed away from the grave and the watching eyes. He knew it had to be an animal and yet...and yet, he hurried to get back to his car.

Inside, with doors locked, he sat behind the steering wheel and tried to think things out. He was covered in blood, he'd been gone for hours, what would he tell Ronny?

An idea hit him and he took the knife out of his glove compartment. Clamping his teeth he sliced his forehead, his shoulder and his arm. The cuts were slight, but bloody. He tossed the knife into Starlynne's garden, and then drove about a mile down the dirt road. He fastened his seatbelt, closed his eyes and grasping the steering wheel in a white knuckled grip, drove off the road into the trees.

The car bounced and jerked, and with a metallic crunch, stopped short. He was shaken up but not hurt. He let out the breath he'd been holding, and ignoring the burning sting of the cuts, walked back to Ronny's cabin.

Ronny was horrified. "It's all my fault, the day was too tiring. You never should have gone out again"

"No, Ron," Dennis said cleaning his cuts. "It's just an accident."

"I'll go get Starlynne, she'll heal you!"

"Dennis turned fast and snapped, "Oh no, don't bother her. I'm all right, they are only slight cuts, see?"

Ronny grew pale.

"OOPS, sorry." Dennis said. "I didn't mean to make you sick. Go lie down."

Ronny did. Late night settled in on them like a heavy, dark, blanket but Dennis found he couldn't sleep. About five a.m. he heard Ronny get up.

"Hey Buddy, where you going? It's the middle of the night."

"Starlynne needs me. She's hurt."

"Come on man," Dennis said, wondering how Ronny could know anything. "You're dreaming. Go back to bed."

Ronny suddenly looked at Dennis with slitted eyes. He shook his head and said, "All right. Good night."

A few minutes later Dennis heard the door open and then heard footsteps outside. Ronny had gone out after all!

Dennis jumped out of bed and followed Ronny as he cut through the woods to Starlynne's. Ronny started up the steps, and then stopped. Dennis hid in the garden, saw the knife glittering in the waning moonlight and picked it up. He didn't want Ronny finding it.

Suddenly Ronny turned around. He hurried into the forest. Dennis didn't understand how, but he knew that Ronny was going to Starlynne.

Ronny headed straight for the grave. He stopped before it and in the dim, dawn light, Dennis saw an unbelievable sight. There, where he had buried her body, Dennis saw flowers. Hundreds of tiny, bell-shaped flowers were growing in the shape of a human. A small human about the size of Starlynne.

Ronny sank to his knees and wept.

"I didn't do it on purpose, Ron," Dennis said coming up behind him. "It was an accident."

Ronny turned, "You raped her, took away her healing powers and she's dead! She didn't have to die. You could have saved her!" Ronny jumped up and tackled him to the ground. "Damn you Dennis," he cried putting a strangle hold to Dennis' throat. "Damn you to Hell. You murdered her!"

Dennis shoved Ronny back, trying to break the grip on his windpipe. Ronny suddenly had the power of a weight lifter. Dennis' air was cut off. With desperation Dennis drove the knife he had forgotten he was holding into Ronny's chest. Both men grunted as blood tricked down the knife handle and down Dennis' arm. He lay there for a moment, too stunned by what he had done.

Ronny was dead. Dennis looked into his unseeing eyes. Revulsion pumped adrenaline through him, washing away the shock. Sitting up quickly, he pushed the corpse off him and bellowed with frustration.

"Things like this don't happen to real people!" he screamed as he staggered away from the body.

"Starlynne was right, I am a killer! No, I'm not. I'm not bad, I'm not! I didn't do anything but react! They both did this to themselves! I'm not bad!" Dennis paced like a wild man and babbled hysterically.

"I'm the victim here, yeah, that's right, me. Well, I'll show them, yeah, I'll make sure no one ever knows about this!"

Dennis ran over to Starlynne's grave, fell to his knees and started pulling out all those damned little flowers. "Grow back all you want, you little bastards. No one will ever see you," he mumbled wildly, yanking out handfuls of the wildflowers and flinging them away. "These flowers aren't going to cause me any trouble, nope. They can grow back till hell freezes over. I'll keep ripping them out. Starlynne, you're dead and you're gonna stay buried!"

Jumping up, he grabbed the shovel he'd thrown down earlier and buried Ronny next to Starlynne. "Well, Ronny you said you wanted to be with her forever," he mumbled laughing at the irony of it all. "Now you have your chance."

The sun wasn't quite up when he finished. The horse-flies were starting to buzz around his head and sweat was forming at his hairline. The bushes to his right were rustling and he saw a shadowy shape moving deeper into the thick woods.

"Hey," he yelled. "Hey you! Come back here!" He dropped the shovel and ran after the witness. "Christ, Oh God, somebody saw me! Please God, don't make me have to kill anyone else. Please!" He pushed his way through thick brush and brambles, tearing his clothes and cutting his skin. He had to find that witness!

Suddenly he felt chilled goosebumps on his arms and the hair on the back of his neck tingled. He stopped and looked around. He saw trees, just trees. And yet…he was being watched again. He was now the one on the defensive. Shuddering, he turned and ran back through the woods, back to the clearing.

Panting, his chest aching, he was stopped by a sound. It was a voice calling his name. "Dennis, Dennis, Dennis," the words repeated, then added, "Buried alive … bleed to death … murder."

"Show yourself, you bastard!" Dennis screamed at the dark woods surrounding him. "Tell me what you want? Goddamnit, I've said I'm sorry! It wasn't murder, I had no choice!"

He saw movement, a figure at the edge of the trees. They were all going to have to leave him alone, he thought. He had to make Ronny and Starlynne understand that it was all a horrible accident. He had to make them leave him alone!

The sun was up and in the pink glow of dawn he saw those tiny white bells back over Starlynne's grave and a heartier yellow blossom covering the shape of Ronny. Their flowery arms were outstretched, hands joined.

Dennis stepped over to the graves and looked down, then over at the man shape at the woods edge. "Who are you?" he yelled.

As if in answer, vines slithered out from the flowers and twisted around Dennis' feet and legs rooting him to the spot. "Hey," Dennis bellowed, struggling against the plants. "Let go!" He pulled, tried to lift his feet, but couldn't break free.

The witness left the trees and approached. "Who are you?" Dennis screamed, his knees weak, his heart pounding wildly. He searched in vain for some way to get away. He went to grab the vines but discovered they were full of thorns.

The figure neared and Dennis saw it wasn't quite human. He stared with absolute terror at the bat-like wings and hoof feet. He fell backwards, the vines pinning his feet to the ground. "Who the hell are you?" he shrieked knowing it was futile.

The creature stopped in front of him, silently looked toward the flower-covered bodies. Then it reached for him and answered in a gravelly voice, "Just a friend of the family."

THERE WILL ALWAYS BE HELL TO PAY

Hilda felt a wave of dizziness sweep over her. She shook her head, trying to clear it, trying to gather her thoughts, to figure out where the hell she was and what she'd been doing.

She looked around a large room filled with empty chairs, and, oh my God, a coffin. She suddenly had that really-bad-pain-in-the-gut feeling as she approached the opened box.

She stood a moment, afraid to look down, but knowing that she had to do it. She forced her head down and stared into her own waxen, dead face. She took in the bad make-up job, the fact that she was in a shroud instead of street clothes, and saw stitches holding her cold stiff lips together and her eyes shut.

She felt like fainting. She reached out and noticed that she didn't have a hand; in fact she was just a wispy smoky thing. So she hovered over her dead self and wondered, *what now?*

"Well the best thing to do, Hilda, is wait and enjoy the show . . . and knowing you, it is going to be a good one," a voice behind her said.

Hilda spun around and saw a thing next to her. It was hairy, grotesquely ugly with short tusks, a misshapen stunted monster's body, and goat legs.

"Huh?" was all she could manage.

"Still disoriented I see."

Hilda nodded, knowing instinctively that she had nothing to fear from this monstrosity. "Pardon me, but who the hell are you to interrupt me in my moment of despair," Hilda sniffed with disdain.

"Good, Hilda, good. The shock is beginning to wear off. In a little while you'll be your old self again," he commented and looked down at her body.

He shrugged. "Well almost your old self. Man, that body is beyond road kill. When you do yourself in, you really do yourself in. I bet there isn't an unbroken bone in that body. Shit girl, you're flat as a waffle and have enough tread marks to look like one, too."

Hilda eyed herself. "I do look a little deflated, and I vaguely remember having a tremendous set of tits."

The creature nodded vigorously. "Sure did, an unbelievable shelf."

Hilda smiled at the compliment, then added, "And who did my make-up? A whorehouse mortician?"

"That's my girl!"

"Your girl? I think not. I'm no one's girl. Whoever I was, I know I have always been my own woman."

The demonic-looking monster smiled, his fangs glinting scummy yellow in the light of the tall, tapered candles glowing at the head and foot of the coffin. "Up to a point Hilda, but I guess you'll remember we are all somebody's something."

Hilda tried to shrug, then remembered that she didn't have shoulders anymore. She glanced at her crushed remains and asked, "So what happened to me?"

"Free will," he answered.

The doors at the other end of the room opened and people started filing in. "Good crowd," she noted. "I must have been popular or important, huh?"

"Well . . . popular isn't exactly the correct term," the monster said.

Hilda started to respond but voices stopped her.

"So … Brunhilda bought the big one," a middle-aged man said as he stopped to stare at her body. "Nice to see somebody finally sewed her mouth shut."

"Ned, stop it," a young woman said behind him. "That is in such bad taste."

Ned turned. "So, bad taste befitted her. Too bad they didn't dress her in one of those awful outdated polyester pantsuits she liked. She deserves to spend eternity in bad-taste hell."

Another small clump of mourners followed. "What a bitch. I hope they give the bus driver a medal."

"Yeah, he was a real hero!"

"Brunhilda sure won't be missed, I can tell you that!"

"I hate to speak ill of the dead, but I really am not sorry it happened to her." "Yeah, it couldn't happen to a better person ... and I use the term person lightly."

"What a goddamned bitch. I'm glad she's dead."

"Ding, dong, the witch is dead!"

Suddenly the stream of comments was interrupted by a sobbing woman.

"Come on, Ellie, she wasn't worth your tears."

"But no one is here to mourn her!" the woman sobbed. "It seems like everybody in the whole world hated Hilda."

"That's right, Ellie, everyone did. She was probably the most hateful bitch any of us have ever worked with. Face it, the woman had no friends and she probably ate her family years ago."

Hilda had heard enough. "Doesn't anyone like me?"

The creature smiled and shook his head.

"Was I really that awful?"

The creature nodded. "And that is why we love you so much. Now follow me Hilda, it is time to go home."

Hilda backed away. "Home? Do I live with the likes of you? Where the hell is home?"

The creature touched her formlessness and they popped out of the funeral home and into the bowels of Hell. "Not where the hell is home, Hilda. Rather, home is where Hell is."

Hilda shuttered, "I'm in Hell? I'm damned?"

"Look Hilda, you are not just damned, you are damned good. Why, baby, you are the best of the worst."

Hilda shook her wispy head and muttered, "I wish I could remember!"

"You will, just give it time. In the meanwhile, why don't you just reacquaint yourself with Hell. You've always enjoyed yourself here before. Sort of like a vacation between jobs. And this time, you deserve a bonus. Not only did you make everyone up there unhappy, you drove five of them to homicide! Five souls transferred to our side! You really are the greatest!"

This last line was uttered with such awe and respect that Hilda felt herself beaming despite the fact she didn't know what she had done to deserve it.

"Murder? I drove someone to murder?"

"Sure did. You were waiting at a traffic light and having quite a discussion with your coworkers when all of a sudden the five of them, yes five, shoved you in front of that bus."

A vision flashed before Hilda: there she was, smiling at the five coworkers, telling them that she held their careers in her hands. They were hers now because she had caught them at a bar instead of the seminar they were supposed to be attending.

To anyone else this might have been a minor infraction, but to the office troublemaker it was a loaded gun. She could manage to twist the entire event out of proportion and even get them fired.

Hilda nodded to herself. The creature was correct--she was very good at what she did. "So tell me, who are you, Satan?"

The misshapen thing laughed. "Badness me, no. I'm just a minion from Hell."

Hilda frowned. "An underling? Is that all I'm worth?"

"Hey, now. I'm almost a major demon, Hilda, and, need I add, your superior in rank. I'll forgive you your insubordination due to your condition, but watch it. You may be one of our best operatives but you still need to tow the line, especially here in Hell."

Hilda sniffed with obvious distaste. "Do I even like you?"

The demon laughed. "Oh Hilda, dead or alive, you really are the bitch!"

Another vision flashed before Hilda: she was yelling at a young woman in an office setting and the girl was sobbing.

Then another vision: she was talking to her neighbor. "I don't want to be a gossip and I promised Sally I'd never say a word, but I felt you should know. Mary told Sally that you are putting your house on the market because this neighborhood is too working class for your tastes and Sally is very upset that you feel that way about everyone who thought you were all friends." Hilda saw the look of annoyance cross the woman's face. "Of course, I don't believe a word of it, but you know you ought to watch what you say around certain people. Not everyone is your friend."

She watched the woman storm off then turned and knocked on Sally's door. "Hi Sally, I was just talking to Gail and she upset me so much that I just had to see you. She told me that Cynthia down the block saw your husband having a drink with Theresa. Now I'm not one to gossip, but you know other tongues are wagging and I just though you should know. Oh please don't cry, dear, I'm so sorry I seem to have upset you."

Another vision, another neighborhood, then another vision and another workplace. Her memory was definitely returning. In every instance she was the center of the action, stirring it up, intimidating people, making life in some way miserable for others.

Somehow she knew that this was right, that this was her lot in life, if not that life then another life because, although she couldn't recall it, she felt she'd been dead a lot.

"So what am I, a ghost? A demon?"

"You, Hilda my pet, have been the biggest pain in the ass anyone in this modern world has ever experienced," the demon told her.

This made Hilda swell with pride. "Yes . . . it's all coming back to me now. That's my job . . . my . . . why . . . my calling. I'm that person everyone dreads. I'm the back-stabbing, troublemaking, vindictive, cunning creep that inhabits every workplace, organization, school or neighborhood!"

"Yep, you got that word for word from the ad, but that's what you do and this time you really outdid yourself. Anytime a job ends in murder, it ends well!" the demon said. "But you got yourself terminated early, and that makes the boss angry . . . you weren't done at that place and now we have to replace you." The demon scratched his groin, shoving his hairy balls this way and that, then responded, "Hilda you have to stay here for a while. Yes, that's the best thing for now."

Hilda glowered at the demon. "And just who are you to decide my fate, I demand to speak to Satan!"

The demon reddened. "Hilda, watch yourself. We like you, but remember how unlikable a person you are. Mind yourself, or it's back to shoveling the fire pits."

Hilda opened her mouth, then snapped it closed. Finally, she sputtered, "I want to hear this from Satan."

"Only demons speak to His Evilness. And although you may be the closest thing to hell on Earth to many people, you are still part of the mortal realm. Demons, as you may well have forgotten, are born, not promoted. You need to go through life from start to finish as a minion from Hell to become a full demon."

Hilda frowned and said, "Oh yeah, now I remember. If I remember correctly, I put in for that twenty-five decades ago. Where's my place on the list?"

The demon walked over to a computer tablet that appeared in a ball of fire. He tapped out a few keys and said, "You are getting close. Six more undisrupted existences and you're in."

"I've got to go back six more times to create havoc and mayhem? That will take more than four hundred years!" Hilda whined.

"I don't plan to wait," Hilda muttered. "If I got myself killed one time, I can do it again."

"All right," she said to the demon, "send me to my next assignment. The sooner I start the sooner I get done."

"Hilda, there is no place for you right now. We need assistant trainers so you will report to the training center immediately."

"Why can't I be a trainer? I am management material, not assistant fluff," Hilda huffed.

"Because only demons train! Now go!" The demon snapped his fingers.

Hilda suddenly found herself facing another demon, a humpbacked gargoyle, as hairless as the last one was hirsute. Gray-skinned and wrinkled, the creature waved his tail in agitation. "Well," it snapped, "I don't have time to train an assistant. I need an assistant for that. Now watch yourself and your behavior. I am having enough trouble with these stupid human souls as it is. Go fetch me a cold coffee."

Hilda stared at the demon with utter loathing. "Yes, your vileness. Don't worry about a thing. I can handle anything and I don't believe a word that other demon said about you. Don't worry; I'd never repeat what that other demon said. I know it couldn't possibly be true. Why you don't have a good bone in your body and I think he was wrong. You are far, far uglier than he is."

Then she turned to fetch the coffee.

When she came back, her new demon was gone and the hairy one was back. "So you think you are clever, huh? Well, you may be one of the worst people ever created, but you still aren't demon material and no amount of trouble you cause will help you advance. Now go and stay in trouble, but out of my way."

Hilda found herself facing a new demon. Before she could speak, it held up a scaly hand and hissed through a lipless mouth, "Ssso, little misssss, I'm on to you. Just do what I tell you, and no, and I mean thissss, no gossssip."

Hilda shrugged and went to work. After a few months of watching and waiting, she found she had enough dirt on every demon in Hell. She was back to doing what she did best, sneaking, lying, skulking around, stirring it up. "Yes," Hilda said to herself at the end of her shift one day. "Soon there is going to be hell to pay in Hell. All I have to do is wait for my chance."

A few days later, as she was writing up a secret report on the demon from the hellfire pit, her old boss appeared. He stood before her and asked, "So Hilda, whatcha doing?"

"Oh, paperwork for my new boss," she replied and blanked out the monitor.

The demon laughed. "Goodness, but you are a bad liar."

Hilda blushed. "I am not, I'm the best. You just know me too well."

"Whatever," the demon said. "The boss can't decide if you are an asset or a pain in the ass. You just can't seem to stop causing trouble, can you?"

Hilda shrugged. "It's what I do best."

"Well, the boss thinks you are too much of a pain in the ass, so he's decided to get rid of you."

Hilda felt a wave of weakness. "Oh no, please not Heaven! Not that!"

The demon laughed. "Heavens no, they won't have you. No, the boss decided that you are just too important a soul to waste on menial labor so . . so he has decided to move you to the top of the list. Hilda, get ready to be born. Remember, no matter how they fix up the outside, you will be, must always be, a demon child on the inside. You will . . . must always do your damnedest to make everyone around you sorry you were ever born. If you do the life-training correctly and live a good, full life then you will come back here a beautiful demon. No more half-life assignments, no more being an underling. You'll be one of us with only the boss to answer to."

Hilda smiled. "This for real?"

The demon smiled and said, "Think you can handle it? Because there is no turning back now."

Hilda was stuck in a black tunnel. She felt squeezed, compressed and then suddenly free. Voices echoed through her consciousness.

"Oh my god, it's hideous."

"Shut up you idiot!"

"Don't worry, sometimes babies have tails and they work wonders with cosmetic surgery. I'm sure she'll . . . Oh, wait, he'll . . . oh, my god . . ."

Hilda listened to the voices and was having trouble understanding them. With each passing moment her grasp of language faded more. She felt a whack and sucked in a breath. Then she turned to see her reflection in the silvered metal next to her. She took in her gray skin and deformed face and smiled. *Beautiful!*

"Oh good, her . . . its color is improving."

"I haven't seen a baby like this anywhere but the textbooks."

"Shhh, not so loud!"

Hilda opened her mouth to say something, but she suddenly realized she had forgotten how to speak. So she screamed . . . long and loud.

As the last glimmer of linguistic skill left her brain, she understood enough to comprehend the doctor as he said, "Will you listen to the lung power on this baby? That is the loudest cry I have ever heard. Boy, are these parents in for a hell of a time."

Hilda smiled inwardly and then let out another shriek.

A WOMAN SPORNED

Sweat beading on her forehead, Andi reached up and pushed the gray streaked hair off her face. *This heat's so oppressive*, she thought and decided to buy a fan when she drove into town later. In the meantime, she got down on her knees and examined the indoor-outdoor carpeting covering the foundation of the screened-in sunroom.

The earthy smell of mildew hit her like a physical blow.

"Ugh!" She picked up the scissors on the floor next to her and started hacking at the cheap carpeting. As the slit grew, she grabbed the edges and ripped, revealing the concrete floor underneath. She tore violently, grunting with the effort until the entire middle was exposed.

"Just my luck," she snorted, staring at the cracked, crumbling foundation. The musty smell grew, filling the entire area with an awful stale stench. Through the cracks that ran down the middle of the floor from house doorway to screened doorway, she saw fat, black, spongy bumps about an inch high pushing up through the tiny pieces of broken flooring.

"Gross!" She grunted and retreated into the tiny cabin buried in the New Jersey Pine Barrens. Wishing for a drink, a real drink, to get the smell from her nose, she sniffed and swore the scent had followed her inside.

She studied her new home, a sweet, tiny, cedar-shake, one-story

117

house at the end of a dirt road and realized that even with the rotting floor in the sunroom and the air conditioner out of commission, she was still incredibly lucky. She'd only been casually friendly with Janine through Alcoholics Anonymous and now Janine had left her this house.

And what better time than now, when she'd lost her job and couldn't pay the rent on her apartment. Andi smiled at her new home, sprayed air freshener, and then mixed herself an iced tea. Moving to the rocking chair on the front pouch, she listened to the sounds of nature.

Five minutes later, totally bored, she muttered "I wonder what happened to Janine?" She stopped a moment, enjoying the companionable sound of her own voice. "I wish I could thank her. I wish I knew why she gave up a great place like this."

The letter that had arrived with the key in the mail just three days ago had been brief.

It read: "Andi, I know you will love it here and I won't be needing my house anymore. It's yours. Pick up the keys and the deed at my lawyer's office."

Andi, who's rent was three weeks overdue, didn't stop to think or wonder or anything. The next day she loaded her car with her few belongings and drove from the coal-filled mountains of Scranton, Pennsylvania to the totally flat, overgrown pinelands of southern New Jersey.

"So odd," Andi sighed, deciding she was finished with both her tea and communing with nature. She went back to the screened-in room at the rear of the cabin. She sprayed more air freshener, although the room was completely open to the outside, and finished ripping up the fake, green grass carpet.

She gasped. The black bumps had grown in what had to be some sort of record time. They seemed to be reaching up, struggling to break free from the broken floor. The big, fat, fingerlike growths, now several inches tall, looked like the appendages of the Elephant Man if he'd five hands.

Andi shuddered, felt goose bumps crawling up her arms. She edged away, backing into her living room and locking the sunroom door. She couldn't stop shivering, the growths had to be more than nature at its ugliest. She just knew that they had to be something supernatural, something evil. She ran outside to the driveway and stood, confusion and fear blurring her thinking.

After a few minutes, she snorted in annoyance at herself. "Get a grip, girl. So you got something nasty growing out back, so it looks like the yeti hands. I don't understand what is going on, but this is my house now, all mine, and no matter what's happening out there, I'm gonna find out about it."

Squaring her shoulders with an exaggerated motion, Andi went back out to the sunroom. She shuddered and gagged, bile burning her throat. The things were even bigger and more defined. She took pictures of them with her phone, then grabbed her purse and drove to the nearest town. She checked into a cheap motel, charged the room to a card already close to being maxed and walked over to the local hardware and feed store.

She looked at the electric fans whirring, their bright red price tags spinning in their wind and realized she couldn't afford the town prices. She glanced over to the leathery old man behind the counter, "Hi, I'm Andi, I just moved into the cabin at the end of Shawtowne Road. Stupid me, I smelled something bad in the sunroom and ripped up the carpet and to my utter surprise I found these." She showed the photos to the clerk, "Ever see anything like this before?"

He studied the screen for a few seconds then grinned. "Dead man's fingers!"

"Andi frowned, "You're joking, right?"

The clerk called to a guy in jeans and a long-sleeve plaid shirt standing a few feet away, "Yo, George, what do you think this is?"

Andi was almost more fascinated that he was wearing a long sleeve shirt and work jeans in this weather than in his answer. "Henry, you know them's dead man's fingers! Why you wastin' my time?"

"Little lady wanted to know."

She looked from man to man wondering if they were fooling around with the out-of-towner. "What are dead man's fingers anyway? They just grew in a matter of minutes."

"Fungus." Henry answered.

"Fungus?" Andi repeated.

"Yep, mushrooms." George added, rubbing his callous hands together. "Yep, we got a wide variety of fungi better known as mushrooms growing in the barrens. Give the area a couple of damp days and they'll all come out to visit us. Totally harmless, you know, as long as you don't eat them or smoke them."

Andi gave a self-depreciating smile, "Not to worry, not my vice of choice."

Henry held up a paperback book about the local Pinelands. "This book will fill you in just fine, little lady. Whole chapter on the fungi."

Hating to do it, but feeling obligated, Andi took seven dollars from her wallet, gingerly fingered the few twenties left, and purchased the book. She sat on a flat of grain sacks and opened it to the chapter they'd just discussed. Looking at the images in front of her, she laughed, embarrassed and feeling foolish. "Dead man's fingers! Quite the appropriate name isn't it."

Out of the corner of her eyes she saw, Henry hand a bottle to George who took a sip and handed it back. "Oops, sorry ma'am. Local wine. Care for a sip?"

Every fiber within her screamed, No, but Andi decided that she could handle one sip, and she certainly didn't want to appear rude to these two locals.

Taking the bottle, she tried to hide the trembling of her hands as she tilted it and took a drink, a big one. She'd only intended a small sip, but temptation won out. Anyway, it was good wine. "Thanks," she said, regretfully handing it back. She'd been clean and sober for almost half a year and knew that she'd just made a mistake.

Henry smiled with pride, "My vineyard. Here--take a full bottle, a welcome to our town gift. Share it with your friends."

She took the sealed bottle and thanked the men, then headed back to the motel for the night. She stared at the bottle for hours while the TV blared in the background. Share it with friends, he had said. Well, she didn't have any friends. People like her never had friends, people like her were meant to live alone, to be alone. That was why she drank, to keep the loneliness away.

"Not this time!" she snapped and went to bed. Tossing and thrashing, Andi was plagued by dreams of strange, silent men with dead hands who were hiding in the forest around her new home. She woke, sweat soaked although the air conditioner churned out chilled air, and thought about Janine. A loner, a loser like herself, they'd been AA friends, the only person she'd had any emotional connection with, her person of choice to fall off the wagon with. She thought about their deep drunken discussions involving loneliness and futility. About how their dreams had all shriveled and died, the husbands, the kids, the fulfillment that had evaded them both. What had happened to Janine, she wondered. *Was she dead? A suicide?* She hadn't seen her in a couple of months, not since she moved to New Jersey.

Andi now owned the house of a probably dead woman. Too creepy, yet it was the only thing in this world she owned besides her ten-year-old car. The urge to run away was so strong she had to force herself to stay in bed. Turn away from the house and she'd have to live in that car. Not much of a choice at all, she decided, and drifted off to more bad dreams.

Early the next morning Andi drove back, feeling sheepish and yet apprehensive. She parked, went around to the back of the place and looked through the slightly rusted screens. The black fingers had shriveled overnight. They sagged to the ground, deflated-looking black smears on the floor. "Oooh, even grosser!"

She cleaned up the wilted fungi and then washed the unbroken parts of the floor hoping to get the last traces. She stopped for lunch and thumbed through the chapter on mushrooms again. "Amazing! Who would have thought there could be so many varieties of toad-stools," she said, realizing most didn't resemble toadstools at all, but rather malignant tumor-like growths clinging to the sides of mossy rocks and pushing out from under decaying brush.

She spent the afternoon sipping iced tea, wishing it were some-thing stronger, but knowing she should never go that route ever again. She tried to forget about the wine bottle as well as the sunroom with the cracked floor and musty smell, but they just kept nagging away at her. "Maybe I'll tear it down. I could plant a garden of flowers in its place. Nice soil, the smell of roses and gladiolus would drown out the smell of mold forever."

She got up and rushed to the shed to see if she had any tools that would smash the concrete foundation to pebbles. Excitement bubbled through her as she searched the dark dank interior. Finally, she had something to do, something to occupy her empty hours, something to take her mind off drinking and how much she missed it. Suddenly she saw it: a sledge hammer. She couldn't lift it, so she dragged it out in a two-handed grip, carefully walking backwards. She had no idea what she was going to do with a tool that was so heavy but felt sure she'd figure it out.

Back inside the sunroom, she stopped short. Her lips curled down and her nose crinkled up. The smell almost knocked her over. She stared at the new growths standing erect and tall and although she was fighting fear and revulsion, laughter suddenly exploded out of her. She couldn't take her eyes off the newest mushrooms to grace her home. Deep pink, they all looked exactly like penises.

"I have a penis garden growing through the floor of my house!" She laughed so hard, her knees gave out and she sank onto the clammy floor. "My god, I've got body parts taking over my home!" she giggled. "What next? No wait, I don't want to know!"

She jumped up and the godawful smell followed her into the kitchen. She sprayed the can of freshener until it was empty and then sat to read her book on fungus again. She thought her phallic mushrooms would have a cool, creepy name just like the black fingers, but there was no genitalia names listed for them. All she found was that they were a variety of stinkhorn mushrooms, and lord did they stink. She sighed and decided to drive into town again and pick up something for dinner.

Pushing the shopping cart around the small grocery store helped her feel normal. By the time she'd finished, she was ready to face the onslaught that nature was apparently throwing at her. She went back to the hardware store to see if Henry was there. She was feeling lonely and his being old and scarecrow-like didn't deter her. She thought that perhaps the mushrooms had made her feel so strangely horny.

"Hey, Henry, remember me?" she said, "I just inherited Janine Trainer's house. Any tales about the place or the area? Folklore?"

The man rubbed his chin a moment then brightened. "Every inch of the Barrens has some lore attached to it. This town was once five miles that way," he said, pointing in the direction Andi now resided.

"But it moved after a terrible forest fire. Everything was destroyed, but that was a hundred years ago. Some say that the cemetery is still out there, forsaken and forgotten and that on moonlit nights the dead walk, looking for their homes and their kin."

Andi shuddered. "Gee, thanks for the information."

Henry laughed and opened a new bottle of wine. "Well, you asked!" he exclaimed as he offered the bottle to her.

She hesitated, but once again didn't want to be rude. Sipping, she laughed, too. "Guess I did, didn't I."

Henry took the bottle back and took a swig, "Just ignore me. As far as I know, I've never seen a ghost or heard one. Anyway, lots of strange stuff grow and live out here. It's a unique ecosystem. The key to becoming a local is to adapt, adjust and enjoy."

Andi nodded, thinking, good advice, hope I can do it. "Does anyone know what happened to Janine? I mean it is wonderful that she left me her home and all, but she just . . . um . . . vanished."

"Janine was a sweet girl, but an unhappy one. Drank, did drugs. She was lonely and frustrated, and in the end, so morose. I guess she was done trying. The one thing about the pines and the marshes, if you want to disappear, well, it's easy to do and almost impossible to get found. I think she died, but maybe she just ran away. Either way, you got a sweet piece of property and with a little work, that place can be right as rain again. Just remember to buy all your supplies here!"

She sat and shared the bottle until it was empty and her head was spinning. Amazing how it affected her after being sober for so long. She smiled at the man in front of her, hoping for a little action. He smiled back, "Well little lady, it's closing time and the wife's got dinner on the table. See you around sometime."

She walked out trying for dignity and settled for tipsy. Driving home slowly, exaggerating her movements, she was trying to be sober. She was embarrassed, hitting on an old, married man, and she certainly was lousy at attracting men anyway. She thought about how she'd never fit in anywhere she'd lived. She was forty-eight years old and lonely. She'd never known the love of a man, at least not real love. Sex was easy, intimacy proved to be something impossible.

As she drove through the dusk, the deep shadows thrown by the trees darkened the road to night. She started to cry. That was why Janine left her this place, she realized. Janine recognized a kindred spirit, another soul lost in misery. This was a place for the perpetually unhappy to dwell, a home for the wretched.

Drunk and depressed, she left her groceries in the car and went directly to bed, so sunk in self-pity she didn't have the strength to do anything more. The night was black when she woke and she felt inexplicably terrified. Something had disturbed her sleep. She realized that she hadn't locked up, that she was still in her shorts, T-shirt, and flip-flops.

And she was positive that there was someone in the house, someone in the bedroom with her. Sweat ran off her and her teeth began to chatter. Tears mixed with the perspiration. She couldn't move, was surprised that she could breathe, and more surprised that her heart kept beating.

Why didn't whoever it was make a move? The shadows in the corner began to swirl and move closer to her. She opened her mouth to scream but no sound came out. She was absolutely petrified. Waves of dizziness washed over her and she knew she was passing out, but just before she fainted, something velvety soft and gentle brushed her cheek and forehead.

Then all was blackness.

Getting up and ignoring the wine headache, she looked at herself in the mirror and saw perfectly normal.

Rationalizing it'd been a dream, the moving shadows and that caressing touch, she brewed a pot of coffee then realized that it was just too hot and humid to drink the stuff. She downed it anyway craving the caffeine kick, then poured a second cupful and walked into the sunroom. Wincing at the putrid smell, she began laughing again. Of course she hadn't been raped in her bed last night because all the erect pink penises were now gray and flaccid, slumped to the floor. "Men, they were only good for just so long and then . . ."

She wondered what would grow next and didn't really care. She was going to tear down this room once the oppressive heat and humidity lifted. The Barrens could just keep its shrooms to itself. She wanted a garden of fresh, colorful flowers.

She spent the day reading, forgetting about the mushrooms and almost forgetting about the bottle of wine on the kitchen counter. In early afternoon, the sky opened up and the rains came. Then, the heat would build up until it was hard to take a deep breath. After the downpour was over, the gray mist that remained reached from the low clouds to the ground and the rain would begin again, rushing down, pounding on her roof.

This lasted all day and well into the night. She tried to sleep, but the humidity was unbearable. Finally, she took the bottle of wine and a portable lamp out into the sunroom in hope of a breeze and tried to sleep on the dirty, plastic sofa shoved to one side of the screened room. She was tired and uncomfortable, her hair plastered to her face and the sweat beaded up and rolled off her continuously. Still, she was grateful that the rusted screens were strong enough to keep the mosquitoes out. She could hear them buzzing, droning endlessly, trying to get through the mesh to feast on her.

She lifted the now opened bottle to her lips and drank. She wasn't enjoying the wine, but she still drank it. Finishing off the entire bottle, she was so tipsy and miserable that she forgot to be scared of the boogie man she had imagined the night before. All she wanted to do was fall asleep and then in the morning figure out how to get the air conditioner working again.

Somehow the buzzing bugs, the alcohol, and the humidity lulled her into a comatose state and she fell into a fitful sleep. Thunder woke her and her small lamp had burned out. The sunroom was dimly lit by the lamp she'd left on in the living room.

Her eyes adjusted and she suddenly noticed the man. He stood in the middle of the room, over the crack, pulling his foot out of the impossibly small opening. She wanted to faint again, but couldn't. She knew there'd be no escape. He turned toward her and she saw him, gray and naked, but instead of being terrified, the vision of him calmed her. He was so beautiful, perfect.

He stared at her and smiled.

Amazed and not quite understanding what was happening, she smiled back.

The gray man moved to her and she surprised herself by holding out her arms to him. He sat beside her on the edge of the sofa, put his arms around her and hugged. She recognized the gentle velvety touch from the night before. It hadn't been a crazed dream, although this ought to be one. He was soft and yet solid enough to be a real man. Holding her gently, kissing her face, kissing her throat, her breasts, he worked his way down her body. A strong stale odor came off him, but she didn't mind, nor did she care about the oddly musty taste of him. With each kiss, she arched toward him, silently begging for more. She understood with each velvety caress that he was what had been missing from her world all her life. He was what she'd been looking for, waiting for.

She kissed back, with a hunger that was surprising. If he didn't take her now, she'd die and go to hell. She had to have him completely. Then he did, and she moaned. It was the only sound in the room as they moved together in unison, blending together.

And then it was over. He kissed her one last time. She knew a good-bye kiss when she felt one. He got up and touched her face, a gentle, loving caress, his skin mossy to the touch. His fingers lingered, for just a moment longer, then never having spoken a word, he walked back to the crack and slowly wilted. He sank down into the dirt and disappeared as she watched, knowing her heart was breaking for the first time ever.

After a second or two, Andi jumped up.

"No!" she shrieked. "Don't leave me. I love you!" She dug at the concrete, breaking her nails, drawing blood, desperately trying to widen the pathway and get him back.

Eventually, she stopped. Weeping, she groaned, "Oh, help me, it's impossible, but I'm in love with a mushroom man." And despite her tears, she smiled at the absurdity of it. "It figures that something like this would happen to me."

She eventually fell asleep on the floor, her hand resting on the crack, her fingers curled into the soil.

Waking to another gray misty day, she watched the rain fall and noticed mushrooms sprouting up all over the back yard. The humidity was relentless and the heat seemed to steal all her strength. She never moved until she noticed that the crack was a little wider, then she dug at it listlessly, knowing it was hopeless.

Once again she was all alone. She cried most of the day, prone on the floor, mourning all the lost opportunities, the lost loves, the children never born. She wished more than ever that she could find another bottle and drink herself into oblivion. But it took too much energy to even think about it.

That night she lay there waiting, but he never came, nor the night after that.

Weak and hungry she woke on the third day to find gray fuzzy patches on her arms, her legs, and other places where gray fuzzy patches just didn't belong. She struggled to the shower and scrubbed at her skin, cleaning it off, then collapsed on her bed. Waking a few hours later, she saw more gray patches. This time after she scrubbed them off, her skin looked colorless, dull. Two more days, sleeping and showering until it hurt, didn't help at all. She studied herself in the mirror, she could see blue veins pulsing beneath her pale white skin as if it were growing thinner, losing layers.

"I've got to get to a doctor," she sighed, but went back to the damp rumpled bed instead. A noise woke her and she pushed herself up to see Janine, naked and covered in gray fuzz at the foot of the bed.

"They're spores," she said to Andi.

Andi tried to stand, but after five days with nothing to eat, she was too weak. "Oh, how horrible!"

Janine smiled. "Not really. As they leave me and find a new home, they blossom into new life. They are my children. And Andi, I have thousands of children. My life finally has meaning. You think this place is for the lost and the wretched, but you are wrong. I left it to you because this place is fulfillment. Don't let it slip away. Come with me. Come finally live your life."

Andi glanced down at her own arms and legs and saw that they were fully covered in what Janine had called spores. "This has got to be the ultimate fungal infection," she groaned. "I need help. I need the hospital. Help me."

Janine came over and half lifted Andi to her feet. "I'll help you. Come on."

Leaning on Janine, Andi struggled to walk.

Instead of going out the front door, they headed for the sunroom.

Andi shook her head. "No, please, help me!"

"I am," Janine said, and pushed her into the room.

The concrete floor was gone, covered instead with hundreds of mushrooms. Andi fell forward, landing on her knees. She reached up to Janine imploringly with one hand and felt the other one begin to sink into the dirt.

She was being absorbed, her knees and legs swallowed by the ground. Too weak to struggle, she opened her mouth to beg again, but just then, a strong, perfect gray hand reached out of the loam and took her outstretched one.

Andi knew it was his hand and suddenly wasn't afraid anymore. She clasped it back, their fingers intertwining, and felt him pull her down, to live with him under the Pine Barrens forever.

AUTUMN

THE CUTOUT

It had been a cold, windy October and the trees shed their leaves a few weeks earlier than usual. But today the wind was still and the crisp bite in the air tasted like Halloween. It promised to be the perfect evening for trick-or-treaters. The sun would set by late afternoon and as it grew darker I imagined the clouds would skitter across the crescent moon, casting eerie shadows to make the costumed youngsters both shiver in terror and giggle with false bravado.

As I sat at my desk and looked out the window, I wished I were a kid again so I, too, could travel door to door, with my identity hidden and my greedy lust for sweets worn proudly like a badge. But I am an adult, almost thirty years old, so the most I can do is open my door to those junior ghouls brave enough to ring my bell and then share in their fun vicariously.

About three-thirty I had the urge to leave work. I decided I wanted to go to the store for Halloween candy, just in case some kids showed up before my date. I know I romanticize trick-or-treating and Halloween, but I live alone in the gray duplex at the end of Downy Street, the last house right next to the woods so I almost never get anyone to come to my door. I don't blame them, not a lot of kids will brave a spooky street for some cheap candy, so while I was out I stopped by the party supply store to get some Halloween decorations, too. I thought maybe plastic pumpkins lit with eerie colored lights would attract more trick-or-treaters.

I was heading for the pumpkins and light up displays when the wall of silly cardboard decorations caught my eye. I don't know why, but I just had to look through them. *This is dumb,* I thought, as I sorted through the jointed door hangings, and then he caught my eye. He was a paper vampire, not one of those silly caricatures of the Count, but a photographic image. I stared at him, folded in thirds, hanging in a plastic bag on the pegboard wall display, and I swear he looked alive. His deep black eyes stared back with an intensity that seemed to be just for me. I could feel myself blushing. He was so damned handsome. I had to have him.

I've always been an honest person. When my friends tried shoplifting in middle school, I never did. So I'm not sure why, but I not only took him off the wall, I stole him. I walked right out of the store with him under my coat. Call it a compulsion, but something seemed to whisper to me that I was doing the right thing. A shadowy voice in my head told me he didn't belong there at all, he was just waiting for me!

I guess luck was on my side because nobody noticed me. It was as if I was invisible. I smiled as I cleared the doorway, amazed at my bold, daring feat. I knew my fiancé, Jake, would never understand. He would be not only shocked by my new criminal bent, he'd be insulted that I could actually get caught up in an infatuated fantasy with a paper vampire. I could almost hear him snap, "Oh seriously, Brenda! This is ridiculous!"

The whole way home I kept one hand on the steering wheel, and the other on the cutout. I imagined what it would be like if my count were real. I pictured myself running my fingers through his graying temples so dramatically offset by his deep black widow's peak. Shivering, I swear I could feel his response. When I pulled into my driveway, I looked at him in the fading daylight, and realized I'd never be able to hang him outside on my front door where the elements could hurt him.

He belonged inside with me, in my bedroom. Feeling a little silly and yet incredibly aroused, I took him out of my car, out of the plastic bag and unfolded him to his full length. He was life size, about six feet from head to black shiny shoes. There was still no wind, so standing in my driveway, I held him up at his shoulders and smiled at my new acquisition. Living alone does have its advantages, you never have to worry about looking silly.

"Hi, my name is Brenda, what's yours? You new around here? Well this is my rental, wanna come inside for a drink, take the chill off?"

I laughed, how positively ridiculous. The real me would never approach a man and invite him in. The real me, the one that didn't steal or lust after fictional decorations, would never talk to a handsome stranger at all. I took him in and hung him on my bedroom closet door.

As I stepped away to study my cutout count, his grin seemed wider, more inviting. I sat on my bed and felt myself getting warm, hot, as we watched each other. I tingled all over, my flesh craving to be touched by his long, delicate fingers. I lay back, my head on my pillow, and closed my eyes. I could hear him moving, coming to me, promising fulfillment. I wanted to stay there with him all night, or maybe even forever. I could feel him slowly coming closer and I ached for the moment to arrive. I needed him, I was going to explode if he didn't hurry. He reached the bed, the mattress sank under his weight, and I held out my arms wishing I could open my eyes to see my love. But I couldn't, my eyes were sealed by a will greater than my own. His voice, a rumbling whisper, echoed in my head, "Brenda, my love."

Suddenly the doorbell rang. I jerked to a sitting position and opened my eyes. Talk about bad timing. The cutout was still on the closet door and I felt foolish. I must have fallen asleep and dreamed the whole thing. The doorbell rang again and I suddenly remembered my date with Jake. I got up and as I left the room, I rubbed my hand across the vampire's dark suited chest in a lingering caress. "It's all right, Count," I whispered. "I promise I'll be back soon."

I opened the door for Jake and somehow I felt uncomfortable looking him in the eye. "I'll be ready in a flash," I said and turned away from him to go back to my bedroom.

He laughed and said, "Take your time, honey, but remember I'm a starving man."

Usually I'd say, *starving for what* and he'd answer, *for you of course*. But tonight I wasn't in a playful mood, at least not for Jake. He suddenly seemed dull and one dimensional, almost lifeless compared to my paper cutout.

Confused by my new feelings, I ran to my room to throw on my dress. Without looking, I knew those flat cardboard eyes were watching me as I peeled off my jeans and sweatshirt and I knew they were filled with approval. I got so flustered by the very idea that I caught the zipper of my new dress while pulling it up. I needed help and I imagined the Count sliding off the door hook and freeing those material-clogged teeth. My knees got weak and shaky as I almost felt his cold hands on my shoulders and his warm, warm breath on my neck.

"Jake!" I yelled, squeezing my eyes shut. "Jake come here a minute and give me a hand." I spun around and looked at my cutout. He was still on the door, it had only been my imagination again. Yet, his eyes were twinkling, laughing at me. I felt somehow disappointed and at the same time relieved. I couldn't help but wonder if bringing him into my home had been such a good idea. Then that whispery voice told me it was and I stopped worrying.

Jake came in, finished zipping me, then noticed we weren't alone. He took a step backwards and barked in a rough voice, "What's that?"

"It's the Count," I answered in my sweetest tone. "Isn't he just great, I picked him up for Halloween."

"Ugh, he's grotesque!" Jack said with a shudder. "I've never seen anything so evil looking in my life."

"Ah, Jake, what's the matter? Scared of a paper man?" I said, getting annoyed at his over-the-top reaction.

Jake glared at the cutout and I swear the Count sneered back at him. "Throw him out!" he commanded me.

"No!" I was now past annoyed and well into anger.

"That thing is an abomination to humanity. I'm telling you to throw him out!"

"NO!" I shouted. "He's mine! If you don't like him, go home. He can't hurt you from two blocks away."

"I'm getting rid of that thing, then!" He yelled.

Before I could react, Jack tore my cardboard fantasy from the door and ripped my paper Count to shreds. Quickly, he carried the tattered remains outside and dumped them into the trash can at the end of the walk.

As he came back up the sidewalk, I blocked the doorway. "Go home!" I sobbed, heartbroken over the loss of a cardboard cutout and frightened by my own irrational behavior. "I hate you!"

A wounded expression distorted Jake's boyish face. "All right, honey," he sighed sadly. "Call me when you've realized that I've done the right thing. I'll be home waiting."

He left, the dark night swallowing him as he crossed the street.

I sat outside on the steps, crying in the still chilled October evening until the cold overcame my grief. I went over to the trashcan, reached inside, and found it . . . empty. My Count was gone! I wanted to blame it on the wind, but there was none. He was just gone.

My feelings of loss were replaced with a dawning horror. *The Count had gone where?* But I was sure I already knew. I had to warn Jake! I ran inside for my cell and hit automatic dial. I waited for him to pick up the phone but the droning tone just rang on and on. Jake didn't answer. Instinctively, I knew he couldn't answer, would never answer.

Really frightened, I stood in the middle of my living room and wept. Tears slid down my cheeks and I didn't even bother to wipe them. I understood everything and I was crying for both of us, Jake and myself.

A part of me was horrified that my fiancé was gone, dead. But what made me cry harder was the little voice whispering to me again, telling me it was good luck that I had found him in that store, telling me I didn't need a mere man anymore. Scared as I was, I nodded to the phantom voice, acknowledging that what was waiting for me was unspeakable and yet somehow worth it . . . that I was a lucky, lucky woman. Deep down I knew it wasn't good luck at all, hadn't been good luck from the moment I decided to go shopping for Halloween.

Out of the corner of my eye I saw a shadow pass by the window, the one with the broken lock. I remembered that I had playfully invited him into my house, had made a vampire welcome to come inside.

Shuddering, I listened to the tap-tapping at the glass, like the sound bare branches make scrapping the outside walls. *Too bad for me it's a still night,* I thought as I went to change into something a little sexier.

WEATHERALL

Every afternoon, Arrestelle walked through the old cemetery. Every afternoon, Arrestelle watched the leaves fall, twirling downward until they hit the ground with a soft, crackling sound. She listened for the sound of the wind brushing past the tombstones. She listened for the sound of the leaves traveling in packs as the gusts made them skitter across her path, bumping against and rubbing her ankles like crispy-crunchy cats. And, a few days ago she started to listen for the voice calling her name.

On the anniversary of her sixth week of foster captivity, Arrestelle got off the school bus and stood in front of the white clapboard house she now called home. This was the last ditch effort of a failed welfare system to keep a stranglehold on her.

She sighed, turned away from the house and walked slowly toward the edge of town, toward the one place that felt comfortable, the one place where someone or something actually knew her as more than just the new foster kid. Where someone called her by her real name.

The sun was setting earlier now, and the air was nippy. Struggling to zip up her denim jacket, she noting that on top of everything else, she was getting fat. She shrugged it off, thinking that at least these foster people fed her well, and she'd developed quite an appetite since coming north. Must be the fresh air, because for all its faults, the far north had really fresh, clean air and a blue, blue sky. Walking through

135

the woods, she stopped to breathe in the smell of October, an earthy scent that made her want to drop and roll in the colorful leaves, bury her face in the smell of raw nature.

Instead, Arrestelle picked up her pace and hurried to the cemetery. She walked between the weedy plots and half buried stones and waited to hear the voice. She didn't have to wait long.

"Arrestellllle."

She stopped walking and looked around. "Where are you?" The only answer was the wind scattering the leaves. "Who are you?"

This time she actually got a response. "Come. . . ."

Arrestelle looked around and noted that the sky was growing dark on one side, turning grayish purple, but on the other side the clouds were taking on an orange hue. A lone tree stood away from the others: tall, thin, and so bare that even the branches were stunted and gnarled like the hands of a childhood monster.

The voice was coming from there.

Arrestelle hesitated, then went. The closer she got to the tree, the more orange the sky grew. By the time she stood by the tombstone next to the skeletal tree, the sky was on fire, streaked with golds and reds, turning the silhouetted tree completely black.

"Hello?" Arrestelle called in a timid voice, as she tried to study the weathered, almost indecipherable, stone. She squinted at the carved letters in the fading light and made out:

J cob We th ra l, Ju y 12, 1863.

"Arrestelle! Welcome my child, welcome home."

Arrestelle felt a wash of dizziness and grasped the stone. Heat seared her hand and she quickly let go with a gasp and shudder. She turned and ran. Without even thinking, she ran as far into the forest as she could, then fell to her knees gasping until she put her hands on the ground in front of her and puked.

She wished for a cigarette, for a shot of vodka, for some drugs, anything that would make her stop feeling scared and hollow. She knew she was experiencing withdrawal, after all she'd been here well over a month. She'd used up her supply of stuff a week ago and she hadn't made any connections yet, not in this godforsaken state. The woods were getting dark, the trees so thick that they blocked out the fiery sky. She got up, and walked toward what was hopefully home.

The woods thinned and she found the road to town. She needed a smoke, wanted one so bad that she wandered into the town's grocery store. She stood around the counter patting her pockets like she was looking for money. As the clerk lost interest in her and her seemingly futile search, she snaked her hand out of her pocket, over the counter and grabbed a pack of unfiltered cigarettes.

The clerk whipped her head around to stare at Arrestelle, who had pocketed the pilfered pack with practiced skill. Arrestelle shrugged and smiled, "Sorry, I was thirsty. Just wanted to buy a pint of milk but I must have dropped my money."

"Oh that's all right, honey, you just grab a milk and pay me another time. A young girl needs her vitamins and calcium," the clerk said with a smile, then turned to wait on the man who had walked up to the counter with a basket of canned goods.

Arrestelle picked up a milk and called out, "Oh, thank you!" and walked out the door.

She threw the unopened milk carton into the gutter and walked home to the new foster people's house. The porch light was on for her. At least these foster people didn't seem to want anything from her, yet. All foster people seemed to want something from her: work, sex, and some even wanted thanks for their "generosity."

Arrestelle decided a long time ago that no one was ever going to give her anything for nothing. Not the endless line of almost faceless foster people, and not her family, who were only a fading memory or maybe only a fading dream. Arrestelle wasn't sure which anymore. All she knew was that when she was old enough to fall in love she was gonna get married and have kids who would grow up knowing who their parents were.

She entered the house and joined the people for dinner.

"So, Ari, how was your day?" the foster woman said.

"Fine."

"Any homework."

"No."

"Where'd you go after school? The bus brings you home at three-fifteen."

"Nowhere."

The woman sighed and stopped asking questions.

"Ari," the foster man took up the task of making conversation. "Are you making any friends? We want you to be happy here."

Arrestelle composed her face into the perfectly bland mask she had perfected over the years. *Then why don't you give me some money so I can buy cigs and vodka. And I smoked my last pipe three days ago.* She thought back to the voice and said, "Yeah, I've started talking to someone."

"That's good," the foster man said, and smiled. "You'll see, small town life is the answer to your problems. You just needed a break from constantly switching homes and hanging on the mean streets---"

Arrestelle worked her facial muscles to keep her impartial mask instead of laughing at the hick in front of her. *Mean streets! Seriously, no one really talks like this anywhere else in the world!*

". . . has been such a great fall this year and we've been having such good weather."

"Huh," Arrestelle mumbled, realizing she had tuned him out. All she had heard was weather and her attention snapped back to the worn down letters on the tombstone. J cob We th ra l. The second word could be Weather-something.

"I got a homework assignment for next week, we need to research some past family in town and I was wondering if you ever heard of a family named Weather-something-or-other."

The man and woman looked at each other.

After a moment's hesitation, the foster man said, "There was a family named Weatherall here for years, since the town was settled, but they . . . uh . . . they left. Where'd you get that name anyway? Why don't you do the Webster's or even us, we've lived here a long time."

Arrestelle nodded and returned to her normal silence and monosyllabic answers. She snuck a few glances at the bottles sitting on top of the serving table. She'd already emptied both the vodka and gin bottles by her second week here and they had been easy to replace with water. She wondered for the hundredth time why they even had a bar, since they obviously never noticed her switches. *Maybe tomorrow night, I'll hitch a ride to another town and find a guy to buy some vodka,* she decided as she cleared the table.

The next day, through a fine misting rain, she returned to the cemetery to have a conversation with Jacob Weatherall. She headed right for the tree, only this time the sky was bleak and the site silent.

"Hey," Arrestelle called. "Hey, you, Jacob Weatherall!"

She waited through the silence for a moment then continued. "Hey!"

She stood there looking at the almost empty trees and the gray sky that seem to blend in with the gray misty horizon. "Why is this place abandoned? Why did your name scare the foster people? Why did you call me and why the hell are you ignoring me now?"

The mist turned into a pounding rain and Arrestelle kicked at the weatherworn gravestone. A chunk of it cracked off. Arrestelle suddenly lost all her anger and bravado. She turned and ran through the woods to the road feeling cold, wet, and desperately in need of a drink, a cigarette, and some drugs.

She heard a car coming and hunched up against the autumn chill, held out her thumb. Back in the city, that would be an act of futility, but out here in no man's land maybe the bumpkins hadn't caught up to the real world.

The pickup didn't stop, nor did the three SUVs and a minivan. She chuckled despite her discomfort. "Guess soccer moms live everywhere."

She faced toward town and shuffled along wishing for a heavy jacket and a hat. A few minutes later another pickup roared past, hit the brakes, and backed up. A red hunting cap peaked out the now opened window, "Hey you!"

Arrestelle looked up, squinting against the pelting rain. A face appeared from under the hat, a kinda familiar face, and Arrestelle's hopes rose. This was a face from school. "Yeah?"

"Hey, you're that new girl?"

Arrestelle nodded, wondering if they gave driver's licenses to idiots in this state.

"Wanna ride?"

Arrestelle jumped in the passenger side.

"Got heat?" she asked, her teeth chattering.

"Hi, I'm Bob," he said, as he turned the temperature knob and floored the car.

"I'm Arrestelle. Got a cigarette, Bob?"

He reached into a pocket and took out a pack. "Arrestelle? That's a weird name."

Arrestelle lit up, fought off a flash of anger, and inhaled the smoke. "Not where I come from."

"Where's that?" He asked. "You still look cold, want a drink?" He reached into the glove box and took out a pint of whiskey.

She grabbed it and drank straight from the bottle, not even flinching as the bitter burning liquid cascaded down her throat. "I'm from everywhere," she said and took another swig. "Lived all over the east coast, probably in every big city in every state."

"No shit."

"No shit. So tell me, I've been here a month and you are the first guy to speak to me, what is there to do fun around here anyway?"

Bob shrugged. "It's a week night, the bowling alley's open but the leagues are using it till nine. Wanna eat?"

Arrestelle nodded and made sure he saw her as she stripped out of her wet shirt.

He cranked the heat on full and drove for about forty-five minutes to a small roadside ma-and-pa style restaurant.

Shirt back on, they went inside. She let him treat her to dinner. When they finished they went back to the car. The rain had stopped and the clouds were clearing out at a rapid clip.

They drove toward her town when he suddenly gripped the wheel with two hands and jerked it over so they headed straight into the woods. She saw he was following a small rutted dirt road that was little more than a path.

"Hey, Arrestelle, I want to show you something really neat. You're not in a hurry, are you?"

Arrestelle sighed and thought, *little late to ask that question, isn't it Bob*, but she answered, "Nope."

He stopped the truck and took out a flashlight from under the seat.

He got out and held out his hand. "Come on."

She joined him. *What the hell*, she thought with resignation, *I owe him for the dinner and drink.*

They walked hand in hand until they broke through the trees and she saw the cemetery on the small hill just ahead. She groaned, not the cemetery ruse!

She could feel him grinning, they always grinned with macho bravado. She sighed, graveyards seemed to turn teenage boys on. Hell, they always wanted to take her to them for sex.

"Hey," he said, "this old place is haunted, you know."

She perked up, maybe he knew something about this place.

"I heard they buried a murderer out here."

She quietly thought, they always have at least one murderer. "Tell me something real!"

"Yeah, a family of murderers named Weatherall. Seems that for generations they'd marry and then look, no spouse."

"They killed their wives?" she asked intrigued.

"No, that's the weird part, the Weatheralls always married outsiders and then they'd disappear leaving the outsider husband or wife to keep the farm and live there. Oddest thing. See that tall dead looking tree silhouetted against the sky. The last Weatherall is buried there. No one knows why he never married, just lived and died. But some people have said that they can hear him calling them. Heck, we even had tourists hiking around disappear then get found right near here. Sometimes they seem to have changed. A lot. Town finally abandoned this place, said it was too haunted. Want to see his grave?"

They got to the tree and the broken gravestone. "Want to smoke some pot?" Bob asked.

She really wanted another drink or something with more kick, but beggars couldn't be choosers, so they shared a joint then made love on the wet grass. Just as she was starting to feel good about her world, she heard it, "Arrestelle,"

She looked at the stone and the ground beneath her, "Yes?"

"Yes, what?" Bob asked, and tried to kiss her.

She pulled away, "Not you."

"Huh? Then who?"

Arrestelle figured that Bob didn't hear Jacob Weatherall.

They drove back and just as they reached the main street they saw the flashing red and blue lights and people all around with flashlights.

A cop flagged them down. Bob rolled down his window and called, "What happened?"

"A girl disappeared, new kid living with the Howard's. Poor kid, we are starting a search party. Hey," the cop shouted. "She's in here! Hey, kid, you found her!"

Bob nodded, not adding that they'd been together for hours.

Arrestelle got out of the car. "Thanks for the ride, Bob," she called, and followed the cop to the foster people's house. She wondered how they would punish her.

The foster woman ran out of the house throwing her arms around Arrestelle. She didn't even seem to notice Arrestelle flinching away. "Oh. Honey!" she said with a gasp. "We were so worried. You must be so cold and hungry. That boy who found you is such a hero. Come on inside. You need a hot shower and some food."

Arrestelle couldn't believe this display. *Guess they'll punish me out of everyone's sight.*

But they didn't. Arrestelle was rushed to the bathroom where the foster mother turned on the shower and handed her a towel. "I'll have some soup ready when you get out, then you need to get to bed. You can tell us all about it tomorrow."

Arrestelle lay awake most of the night, first wondering why the foster people reacted so strangely and then wondering why she could hear a ghost and Bob hadn't.

The next day it rained and the day after that Arrestelle waited, watching the foster people and wondering what made them act like they cared. Finally, the sun came out on Halloween day. A cold front moved in and Arrestelle walked to the cemetery at a fast pace to keep warm. She sat on the tombstone under the skeleton tree and waited. She shivered and thought about her heavy coat in the closet, the one that was too tight to button. The afternoon faded away into a spectacular blood and fire sunset,

She sat and wondered why she was there and the voice answered her. "To trade."

She opened her mouth but suddenly felt like she didn't have one. She struggled to move but she didn't have anything to move. She wasn't looking up at the sky that had turned from blood red to bruised purple. She realized with a claustrophobic panic that she wasn't on the gravestone any more, rather she was under it, in the earth. She was aware of everything, the clumps of dirt that surrounded her, the roots intertwining her bare, disintegrating bones, the worms that slithered around and through her, the bugs scurrying through the layers of decaying leaves above her, the small animals getting ready to sleep, and the nocturnal animals just coming awake.

But most of all she was aware of herself still sitting on the tombstone. And yet it wasn't her anymore because she wasn't there.

"So, Arrestelle," the her above ground said, looking down toward where she really was. "Confused?"

Arrestelle nodded or at least tried to nod. "Yes," she answered without a mouth. "Yes!"

"Well, from as far as I can tell, and it is all hearsay, we traded places. I'm you and you, well you are a rotten, decaying corpse stuck in the ground until you can find release."

"Huh?" Arrestelle said, "Why'd you do this to me?"

"Because I could. I've waited three decades until you showed up. I was actually afraid no one would ever come."

"Why me?"

The teenaged girl sighed. "Look, it takes a few things to happen. It has to be autumn, preferably late October, it has to be sunset, and it has to be family."

Arrestelle felt awash with confusion and anger. "This is stupid! Autumn, sunset, family? Who made all this up, you?"

The girl above her laughed with her voice, "No, I guess it must have been Jacob and some deal he made."

"You're Jacob!" Arrestelle interrupted.

"No, now shut up and I'll tell you. Jacob was a few Weatheralls ago. I wasn't the first to stumble onto this trap and the story has been handed down to me, sort of a whisper down the lane. I came here thirty-five years ago to find my New England roots. Whoever came before me, some other Weatherall, convinced me I was some kind of psychic and he had me coming back constantly feeding me lines of bullshit until I arrived on a late autumn afternoon and then poof, he got out and I got stuck in the ground. Old Jacob and his clan never planned to die at all, just found a way of continuing."

"What's that got to do with me, I don't have roots anywhere, and I certainly don't have family."

The girl rubbed her face and hair and laughed. "Wow, I'm young and being a girl is really strange, but then again, it has been so long since I was a man that I almost forget what that was like. I was fifty when it happened and now I'm a teenager. Well, I certainly know how to use the years now. No more wasted youth. You've been quite the abuser, haven't you, but it is not too late to reverse your damage."

"What about me!" Arrestelle screamed.

"Well, you are a fortunate coincidence for me, you ended up in the one place that could save me, because you, my dear, have Weatherall blood. Not a lot of lineage, but enough to switch. Look, let me give you some advice. When you feel someone, well then that makes them a Weatherall. Get them here at sunset in the fall and poof, you're out and all new, and they are in."

"That's terrible. How could you do this to me!"

"Hey, a few years underground numbs the conscience." Arrestelle's new owner said as she headed away from the grave. "Well, I have to go now, Arrestelle. Hey that's my name now. Anyway, maybe I'll see ya in another life."

Arrestelle wanted to cry. She didn't deserve this. Life had always stunk but this was just too unfair. Then she felt it, a Weatherall, right there next to her. "Wait," she screamed. "Wait! Stop!"

The girl stopped walking away. "Why?"

Arrestelle suddenly knew why her clothes were tight. "You're pregnant!"

The new Arrestelle returned to the grave. "She concentrated. "So I am."

The silence hung there for a few minutes. Finally the switcher said, "You know you can switch."

Arrestelle felt sick. "That's my baby."

"I know."

"If I switch, I . . . I am abandoning her."

"Yes."

"I'd be just like my mom. I don't want to do that."

"I know."

"But," Arrestelle sighed, realizing that if she didn't switch, she'd still have abandoned her daughter because this stranger in her body would be the mother. "This isn't fair at all!"

"No," the switcher agreed. "No, it isn't, but then again, in your case it never has been, has it?"

Sadness covered her like a blanket woven from despair. "No, never fair, why are you doing this, telling me this. Why are you telling me to switch?"

"Guess I feel guilty for doing this to you, stealing your body and all. I'm not a bad person, just a desperate one."

Arrestelle struggled with herself. She'd always promised that she'd be a good mother someday, but how could she do anything for her baby stuck down here in the cold damp ground. Then again, it was her child, a truly innocent soul, and she'd be condemning it to eternity down here if she switched. "Can a baby get out of here?" she asked.

The girl shrugged, "How do I know, I didn't create this situation, I got trapped by it, just like you and if you don't decide in the next minute or so, the sun will be completely down and then it's too late."

Arrestelle didn't know what to do. She saw the sun vanishing and reached out in desperation, switching with her unborn child.

She felt the life around her and reveled in it. "I'm alive again," she said. She searched for the baby's spirit. "Where is it? I wanted to explain to it."

"Explain what? That you thought you were more important than your own child. Anyway, it isn't here," the pregnant girl said. "It's gone, I felt it leave. I think this cursed grave can't hold that which has never lived. The baby returned to where it belonged."

Arrestelle felt her new body, so small, so unfinished. "This isn't right! The heart is hardly beating, the lungs are way too small, and the brain is wrong. This is a bad baby!"

The man who was now the girl who was going to be the mother sighed and Arrestelle could feel the sadness. "No, the baby isn't bad,

145

Arrestelle, you were. You drank, did drugs and ruined this child. But don't worry, I'll take good care of you for however long you live, no matter how defective and deformed you are. I promise."

There was nothing left to say as the final rays of the sun vanished. Settling into the womb and her new life, Arrestelle counted the futile, irregular beats of her struggling heart as she waited to be born into the life she had created for herself.

SCREAMING HALLOWEEN

She spent an hour getting ready—actually she spent the entire year preparing for this one night.

For the thousandth time, she wished she could keep a real glass mirror and for the millionth time she was glad she couldn't have one. It wasn't easy being ugly enough to shatter glass. So instead she held up a highly polished silver serving tray to study her reflection.

"God, I really, really hope that the vision looking back at me is just distorted by the shape of the tray," she muttered because living alone for centuries tends to make one talk to themselves. Sighing, a deep sigh, she dabbed a bit more ruby red lipstick to her dead-fish-belly-white lips and a bit of pink cheek color to her gray skin. Finally satisfied, she walked down the hundred and fifty steps of the tower she called home and mounted her faithful, but dead horse which she rode it to the nearest village that had train service into the city.

Two hours later she stepped off the downtown train with all the other costumed revelers and headed to the Halloween party at the pub.

As usual she had high expectations.

But then she always did.

She glanced at the refection of herself in the storefront window and took it all in before the glass shuddered and shattered. Despite having a face that could scare someone to death, she knew, without a doubt, she had a rocking body, in fact a body to die for. That face and her wild, white hair, her marvelous hair that could rival Medusa when it came to writhing, well, that was a different story. But it was Halloween and she was at a costume party.

She entered the bar and looked the place over. Immediately she saw him and her heart fluttered. She smiled at him from across the room and he smiled back. This time she was sure, "My one true Love!" she called without fear of being heard over the music.

Then like magic he was by her side. They danced for hours and drank drinks with funny names and big kicks.

By midnight they were back in his room in bed together. "Wanna wash off your make-up?" he asked.

"Not now, why don't you just turn down the lights?" she answered in almost a whisper.

He did and in the dim glow of the streetlight outside, he kissed her.

She kissed him back with the hunger of a year of pent-up lust. "I gotta warn you, I'm a real banshee," she told him when she came up for air.

"Not to worry. So was my last girlfriend. She liked to scream, too. I'm good with it."

With a sad smile she thought, *yeah that's what they all say, but maybe this time …*

They made love and although she tried not to, at climax she screamed like the banshee she was, and he screamed in pain as blood gushed from his nose, ears, and mouth.

She got up, got dressed, and turned on the lights to look at his limp body. She sighed, overwhelmed with regret and shed a single tear. Nudging his lifeless body with her toe, she muttered, "Yeah, that's what they all said. All of them. Oh well, guess this will have to hold me until next Halloween."

BETWEEN FEAR
AND MADNESS

Jen sat in her dorm room gazing into the magnifying mirror. She knew she should be studying but she just enjoyed looking at herself too much to quit. She admired her flawless pale complexion, her lovely long auburn hair and she glowed with the inner knowledge that she was more than just pretty. "Gotta start working on my paper, it's due in two days and I'm afraid I won't get an A as usual," she said, knowing that she was smart as well.

She glanced up as she spoke and saw Martha, her roommate, sitting on the bed twirling a strand of her shoulder-length mousy brown hair and glaring at her with an intensity that was downright scary.

Jen met the stare for a few seconds, then broke away, lowering her eyes with a shudder at the fierceness behind her roommate's eyes.

"What?" she asked, looking up again but not meeting Martha's eyes. She knew relations between them had been strained lately, so Jen was surprised that Martha didn't make a sniping remark.

Instead she said, "You know, I haven't talked to my mother in a long time."

Jen nodded. "Yes, I know, and I just don't understand how you can shut out your parent like that! It's wrong, just so wrong."

Squinting her eyes, Martha snapped back, "That's right, you just don't understand! And I don't have to explain it to you. That woman treated me like shit. Shit! I've hated her for a long time."

Jen nodded again. "But she's your mother, you have to love her, too."

Martha suddenly smiled, and Jen could see the stiffness and anger flowing out of her. "I do love her. She's my mom and I've decided that I am going to finally forgive her. I'm going to go see her."

"Now? Tonight?"

"Of course not tonight. Tomorrow. Hey, it's like eleven and it's Halloween. Let's go check out the old haunted house on Purgatory Road. I bet one of the frats is having a party out there."

Jen shuddered. "Are you serious? You know all those people died there. Murdered in their sleep back when it was a nuthouse."

Martha laughed. "That was fifty years ago. And besides that place burned down."

"Yeah," Jen said in a quiet voice, "and I hear that the property is haunted by dead, crazy spirits."

"I betcha all the crazy ones are long gone, but it doesn't matter. It's Halloween, time to go find us some ghosts. I heard they rebuilt the place as a museum. Come on, let's go see."

Jen fidgeted. "I didn't hear about that. When did they do all that construction?"

"Over the summer. Anyway, who cares?"

"Hasn't been any talk about it."

"Seriously, Jen, like I said, who cares? Let's just go there. Be adventurous for once. Grow a damned spine for Chrissakes!"

Jen grimaced. She hated being scared. But everything scared her. Bugs, lightning, movies, noises, even being scared frightened her. Name just about anything and she could find something to be afraid of about it. She squared her shoulders because Martha was correct, it was time she got some backbone. After all, she was nineteen and didn't really believe in ghosts. At least not much anyway. "All right, but I'm not going to get out of the car unless there are lots of people there."

As they walked to Martha's car, Jen shuddered and said for probably the hundredth time to Martha since they became roommates, "I can't help being afraid. It's just the way I am."

Martha laughed. "Well, that's your problem. Me, I've never been afraid of anything."

Jen nodded in agreement at that and wondered what kind of trouble Martha was going to get them into.

Martha drove through the university and headed to the outskirts of town. When she reached the faded street sign that read Purgatory Road, she turned down the rutted dirt road that dead-ended at the asylum. Steering with her left hand, she turned and looked at Jen saying in one long gush of a run-on sentence, "Interesting story, that nuthouse, I'm sure you know that one of the frats from this school sent six guys over there as a pledge stunt and they let lose a locked up homicidal inmate who went on a rampage and killed all the other fifteen inmates, the doctor on duty and three nurses."

Jen nodded, "I've heard that."

"And then the frat guys burnt the place down to cover up what happened, so now the place is supposed to be haunted," Martha finished.

"Yeah, I knew that, but you just said back in the room that it's been rebuilt as a museum. Is that supposed to be haunted now?"

Martha laughed. "Forget the haunted shit. Tell you what, if there's no party out there, we'll go buy some beer after this and get really trashed. We could even sneak into a bar later and meet some guys. That is, if you don't snatch them all first."

Jen hedged, "I don't know. I really need to finish that paper. I can't let my GPA fall or I'll lose my scholarship."

"Always scared of getting in trouble!" Martha sneered. "Stop being such a goody-goody!"

Jen reddened and snapped, "Martha, seriously, who says goody-goody. That's about as old as the Purgatory loony bin. And besides, I don't get all the guys."

Martha snorted.

"Well, I can't help it if I'm pretty," Jen said defending herself, knowing that she damned well reveled in her looks. All she had to do was flash those big, ever-so-slightly slanted green eyes at a male and then spread her perfectly shaped lips into a smile that showed off her dimples and sparkling white teeth and he'd forget every other girl in the place. That was her best talent, and one she wasn't afraid of using at all.

Martha snorted again.

Jen sighed. "Look, I'm sorry about Rob."

"I loved him!" Martha said. "You don't even like him that much."

Jen took a deep breath. She hated confrontation. It scared her. "I thought that was over. You and I, we made up didn't we? Look we're roomies, can't this just be water under the bridge. So he wanted me, not you. That's not my fault."

Martha nodded and Jen saw her smile again. "You're right, Jen. He preferred you. Not either one of our faults. Sorry. Best roomies forever."

As Martha turned down the long leaf-covered driveway to the site of the old-fashioned mental institution, Jen tried to appear calm but she felt the ever so familiar flutter of butterflies in her gut, signaling that she was once again afraid. *Afraid of trespassing, afraid of getting in trouble, afraid of feeling this scared.*

As they pulled up to the front, Jen gasped as the headlights shone on the three story building. Warm yellow light streamed out of every window. "Wow! They really fixed this place up nice!"

Martha opened the car door. "Let's check it out, looks like a party. Maybe a Halloween party! Damn, I wish we'd worn costumes."

Jen remained sitting in the front seat. "I don't want to go anywhere. Let's leave." But she was talking to the air as Martha headed for the big wooden front door. "Wait for me!" Jen yelled, tumbling out in her rush not to be alone. She was shaking, terrified to go in, and terrified of being left behind.

Martha knocked and then smiled as it was opened by a teenaged girl with old-fashioned braids and a below the knee cotton dress in institutional gray. "Can we come in?"

The girl nodded, opened the door wide, and asked, "Could I stop you?"

Martha laughed. "Nope," and led the way in with Jen right behind her.

"Don't leave me," Jen whined. "Don't leave me out there."

Martha turned back and stared at Jen with an intensity that made her shrink back. "No, Jen, I promise, I won't leave you outside. Now follow me."

The door shut. Jen focused on the party going on around her. The room wasn't full but there were about twenty people in costume, dressed like inmates and staff. They stood about silently and stared at the newcomers. "Hi, everyone! It's me!" Martha said, and just about everyone looked fearful.

Jen looked around at the partygoers and then back at Martha. "I don't get it. They know you?"

Laughing like a screeching bird, Martha danced around the room waving her arms wildly over her head. "Hell, yes. They know me. They definitely know me all too well. Executioner, judge, jury, and savior. Yeah, they really know me."

The large grandfather clock against the far wall chimed twelve times. Martha still jumped around to music no one else heard, looked over at Jen and said. "Hey it's tomorrow."

She finally stopped dancing around in front of a stooped over man with thin gray hair, a face full of warts, no teeth, and a bulbous nose. "Hey, Mom, I've come to forgive you for putting me here."

The man shied away, cowering against the wall.

"I said I forgive you so you better be happy."

The man picked at an open sore on his creek, gave a forced gummy smile, but said nothing.

Martha smiled back then danced her way over to Jen who was backed against a wall. "He doesn't talk much. Guess he's got nothing to say. Too bad, huh?"

Jen shook her head from side to side. She had no idea what was going on, but there was something very wrong. "Why are you acting like this?" she whimpered.

Martha grabbed at Jen's hands, but Jen yanked them away from her. "Stop it now, Martha! You're scaring me!" she yelled, pushing herself tighter against the cold plaster wall as tears streamed down her cheeks. "This is some sort of trick and I hate tricks so just cut it out. I mean it, cut it out right now and let's go. You and your friends have had your damned fun."

Then Jen forcefully pushed herself off the wall and started to take a step toward the door when Martha reached out and gently took a strand of red hair. She twisted it around her fingers, like she did to her own hair and laughed that deranged laugh again.

"Oh Jen, you aren't going anywhere, not just yet. Such pretty hair, such a pretty girl. Oh, I was so jealous, but not anymore. Not anymore."

She dragged Jen to the old man, who still cowered against the wall. "Mom, come take my hand. Time for a personnel change. It's been a while since the last time, huh, boys? But don't get excited, it's not gonna happen for any of you."

The old warty man took Martha's hand and then Martha clutched Jen's hand in a cold iron grip. Jen tried to pull away but couldn't. She started crying loud, gulping, sobs, while clawing at Martha's hand with her nails.

"Stop that, Jen, you'll hurt Mom," Martha said and giggled.

Jen yelped, feeling more fear than she had ever experienced before. She felt the air die in her lungs as she tried to breathe. The room began to spin wildly, the lights flickered, all noise ceased, and Jen felt an intolerable hollowness and a melancholy and a loneliness so engulfing it overwhelmed all her other senses. She was being ripped to pieces and put back together with emotions she'd never experienced before.

Then it stopped. Jen could finally take a deep breath only she couldn't breathe at all. She was dizzy, like after riding the Tilt-O-Whirl.

As the vertigo settled, it was replaced with a feeling of bewilderment. She tried breathing, but it still felt wrong. She was now cowering against the wall, but that, too, wasn't right.

She stared around the room with blurred, clouded vision, and screamed. Vomit tried to fight its way up her throat and a cold sensation started settling on her like death itself as she looked from person to person, taking in each chalky white face and knowing immediately, that everyone in the room was very obviously dead. The young girl who had let them in had a knife buried in her back, her dress red with blood. As Jen took in each person, she could see that they all had fatal wounds.

And dead as they all were, they smiled sad little smiles at her. Pitying smiles.

Jen shifted her eyes away from those dead faces, and found herself squinting through cataracts at Martha and at herself. The dizziness returned and she collapsed against the wall and slid down to the floor.

Stepping back and away from her, Martha took Jen's hand, only Jen couldn't feel it. In panic she discovered she couldn't feel anything, not herself breathing, not her hand being touched. In fact, she realized she was watching Martha and what had been her physical body from a distance. They had both moved away from her vantage point so that she was still propped against the wall, but now she could see Martha and herself half a room distant.

Everything felt so surreal, Jen wondered if she'd been drugged, maybe tripping. She watched herself talk, listened to her voice coming out of the mouth on her face, and yet she wasn't speaking.

"Sorry, Jen," Jen's mouth was saying. "But I figured Mom has spent enough time repenting for putting me in here all those years ago. She's sorry for calling me crazy. Well, maybe I was crazy, so crazy that I killed everyone when those boys opened my cubicle. But I made it up to all of them. I got everyone I hurt new bodies."

Jen shook her head. "I don't understand."

Jen's face smiled at her. "Always thought you were so smart, didn't you. Always making Dean's List, always afraid of not getting the best grades. Bet you feel pretty dumb right now. Don't get anything do you?"

Jen just silently shook her head.

"Let me make this simple for you," Martha/Jen said. "I was crazy once, I killed everyone here, and I've been body switching for the last five decades. You see, crazy does have its good points. It made me able to switch. Didn't know it at first until some dumb kids came here the Halloween after the fire. Anyway, I went to scare them, touched one of 'em and the next thing you know, we switched. I was the only spirit here who could do that, so to make up for all I did bad that awful night, I helped all the other doomed spirits stuck here to get a life. I came back every Halloween with a few friends until the switching was all done."

Jen licked her lips and shuddered. She had no teeth. "Why'd you do this to me?" she asked. "I thought we were friends!"

"Martha shook Jen's body's head making her beautiful ginger hair sway from side to side. "Yeah, Jenny girl, just great friends. Basically, I only come back here now when I want to be a new person. Fifty years in one body gets old, so every couple of years I bring someone here so I can freshen up."

She stopped to laugh, then added, "Or like when someone needs to be punished, you know, someone like you, Jen. Well, I put them here for a while. I decided I've punished Mom enough and I needed a live vessel for her, and since you took Rob from me, I figured I could just take your body and have him for myself. I gave Mom my current body, not so pretty, but young and firm."

"Come on, Mom," the body that had once housed Jen continued as she led what had once been Martha toward the outside. "You're going to love the twenty-first century."

Jen touched her face and felt the warts, the sores, the huge nose, and then the tears as she wept. Standing up in her new old, stooped ugly shell, she watched Martha, now inhabiting Jen's body and Martha's mother now in Martha's body, leave the old asylum. The building lights died and her old filmy eyes adjusted to the dark, She watched through the burnt out window frames as the car lights pulled away.

"The building wasn't rebuilt at all," she mumbled, trying to grasp on any fact that was real.

"No shit!" one of the ghosts said.

Jen looked around at all the spirits beside her.

"Don't worry, you sort of get used to this," one of the others said to her. "She's been switching with the living for decades. Sort of a payback for the massacre that happened in the sixties. Right Tommy?"

The little girl with braids snarled. "Yeah, she got all six of us from the pledge group that night to come back here and then made us trade places with six of the ghosts. The ultimate retribution, I guess. The insane back out in the real world, and the perpetrators stuck back here."

"But I had nothing to do with the fire, the murders!" Jen wailed. "I'm not insane!"

"Maybe not, but you sure pissed her off. So welcome to the club and cheer up, because every once in a while she comes back, does a switch and releases someone. That is, of course, after she feels that enough time has been served."

Jen stared at the girl with the braids. "How long have you been here?"

A ghostly tear ran down the girl's cheek. "I'm a lifer, all of us who actually caused that disaster back in the day will never be freed. She made that perfectly clear to us."

Jen nodded and now understood that all her fears, a lifetime of being scared was nothing compared to the decades, maybe even centuries of maddening emptiness that was facing her. Finally free of irrational fear, she was now condemned to join the spirits haunting the madhouse on Purgatory Road.

EVERYBODY'D EAT STEAK

Eloise O'Banion leaned against the white wooden railing that encircled her porch. She watched the dying summer blooms waving their withered heads at the children as they walked and skipped past the old Victorian house.

"I wish," she mumbled. "I just wish." She shook her head covered by thin bluish-white curls and sighed deeply once again. "If wishes were fishes . . ."

Turning away, she grasped her walker with tight fists of anger and hobbled stiffly over to the wicker rocking chair. She backed painfully into the seat and slowly relaxed, watching the boys and girls make their way to the school two blocks away.

Here it is, the last week of September and everyone is on their to school, she thought bitterly. *Everyone except me.* She felt tears of frustration slide from her eyes and work their way down the network of wrinkles that were her cheeks. Embarrassed by this display of frailness, she let the tears stay, rather than wipe at them.

"I'm only sixty-nine," she said to the dove splashing in the birdbath on the front lawn. "If I weren't so handicapped, I'd be with my new class right about now. Instead they retired me with a thank you and a luncheon. Is that fair?"

Too depressed to enjoy the warm September sunshine, she slowly pulled herself up and inched her way into the house. She put on the kettle for tea and then sat and waited for Mrs. Hillery who was due at 9 a.m. Eloise shuddered at the thought of the old biddy coming over to help her. "Imagine coming to this," she muttered. "A nurse-maid in the guise of a housekeeper." She sighed heavily once more. "I wish I didn't have to put up with any of this nonsense!"

A sparkle outside the window caught her attention and she turned to see what it was. Coming through the fluttering yellow curtains was a platter-sized globe filled with glitter like the children used on holiday decorations. She watched as the sparkling bubble touched the floor, gaping dumbly as it exploded in a shower of gold confetti.

There, on the checkerboard linoleum, stood a beautiful young woman. Feeling more curiosity than fear, Eloise studied the intruder, taking in the layers of taffeta on the white and pink dress, the gossamer wings sprouting from her back, the long strawberry blonde hair topped by a jeweled tiara. She decided that the bubble and woman were too absurd to be a threat and said, "It's terribly rude not to knock, my dear."

The apparition waved a silver wand complete with a large star and said, "I am your fairy godmother, Eloise O'Banion, and I heard your wish." The lovely fairy stopped and stared at Eloise in shock. "Oh my stars, Miss O'Banion! I thought you were dead!"

"That's a nice way to greet your old fifth grade teacher, Mary Margaret Holmes!" Eloise snapped. "I always said that you were a flighty girl."

"M-M-Miss O'Banion," Mary Margaret stammered. "I'm sorry, I was just so surprised that I just didn't think."

"Hurrumph," Eloise hurrumphed. "You never did use your head enough. Why I remember how you used to get Tony Lewis to do your homework for a kiss on the cheek. I wonder what ever happened to that foolish boy?"

"He's a store manager," Mary Margaret said, then stared wide-eyed at Eloise. "Why Miss O'Banion, how did you know Tony did my homework?"

"Never mind that," Eloise said, and shifted slightly in the hard chair to look directly at the girl. "Why are you dressed up like Glinda the good witch, and as much as I enjoy visits from my students, why are you standing in my kitchen at eight forty-five in the morning?"

Miss O'Banion, I'm a fairy godmother. Your fairy godmother. I'm going to grant you three wishes."

"Mary Margaret, did you join a cult or did you just get involved with drugs?" Eloise asked in disgust

"No, no, Miss O'Banion. It's my job. I was enlisted in the F-G guild six months ago. You see, I was having a hard time finding a job so I went online to the 'Dreams Do Come True' employment service. Now here I am, gainfully employed. In fact, you're my first solo assignment," Mary Margaret said, as she studied her reflection in the mirror hanging on the wall in the next room.

"You are such a vain girl, look at me when you address me," Eloise said sternly and hid a smile. *Children grow up, but they just don't change,* she thought with an absurd teacherly satisfaction.

"Sorry, Miss O'Banion," Mary Margaret said and looked her directly in her wire-rimmed glasses.

"That's better. Now my dear," Eloise said, "I don't know how you pulled off the bubble stunt. After all, you never paid any attention to your science lessons, but I think you'd better go home now. By the way, how is your dear mother, are you still at home with her?"

"She's fine," Mary Margaret said automatically, then frowned and added, "Miss O'Banion, I really am your fairy godmother and I have to grant you three wishes."

"Mary Margaret, if I've said it once, I've said it a thousand times. If wishes were fishes, everybody'd eat steak."

Mary Margaret smiled, "I remember, Miss O'Banion, I remember." Gazing at her with a perplexed almost cross-eyed look, Mary Margaret said, "I never understood what you meant."

"I know," Eloise said smugly. "You're a nice girl but a little on the dense side. All looks and a little short on the smarts."

Mary Margaret looked hurt. "What does it mean?"

"Never mind, I'm more concerned with your delusions. Fantasy is fine in books, but this is the real world."

"Please Miss O'Banion, this is for real. Make a wish, not a small one, and I'll grant it," Mary Margaret pleaded.

Eloise snorted, feeling bitter and angry. *The nerve of this cruel girl, coming back into my life to taunt me.* Just the thought of being granted a wish filled her with longing and regret. "Young lady, I wish you would leave. Right now!"

In a huge puff of gold fairy dust, Mary Margaret vanished. The sound of her despairing wail echoed in Eloise's ears.

Eloise sat immobile, staring at the spot where Mary Margaret had vanished. She was so lost in thought that she didn't hear the teapot screaming for attention until Mrs. Hillery let herself in.

"Miss O'Banion! My goodness, you'll ruin that kettle," the housekeeper scolded as she fluttered around the kitchen like a hyperactive butterfly.

For once Eloise didn't mind the company, it helped to take her mind off her disturbing visitor. Still, thoughts did creep in. . . . *What if it had been real? Never! . . . But what if I could return to a fruitful life? Stop torturing yourself . . .*

That evening, after Mrs. Hillery made dinner and left for home, Eloise was standing in the hall looking out the screen door when the bubble reappeared. Mary Margaret poofed into being in front of her. "Please, Miss O'Banion, don't say a word," Mary Margaret said in a breathless rush. "You've already wasted one wish. Don't waste another."

Eloise shuffled slowly to the overstuffed sofa set in the corner of her dark living room and plopped down. "I have always secretly worried that a student would come back and haunt me," she muttered, shaking her head from side to side. "All right, Mary Margaret, what will it take to get you to leave me alone?"

A silvery tear trickled down from Mary Margaret's right eye. "Oh, Miss O'Banion, why are you making this so hard? You always were too demanding and strict," she said in a quivery voice.

Anger flared through Eloise, all feelings of despair dissipated, "You impudent girl! First you burst into my home, then you have the gall to criticize my professional techniques. How dare you!"

Mary Margaret held up her hands as if to ward off the verbal blows. "Miss O'Banion, you called for me! You made a wish!"

Eloise saw a gleam appear in Mary Margaret's eyes as her voice softened. "Now, please, Miss O'Banion, don't carry on so. After all, this is my first assignment, and you wouldn't want people saying that one of your students failed in life because of you, would you? You don't want me to be an unemployed failure?"

"Mary Margaret," Eloise said. "After teaching over a thousand students, I'm sure many turned out far worse."

She watched Mary Margaret give up rational debate and start to weep. Giving in, Eloise smiled kindly at the pathetically whimpering woman and said, "There, there, Mary Margaret, stop blubbering. I'll let you grant my wishes, although I don't believe in any of this foolishness."

Her face brightening through the tears, Mary Margaret smiled. "Oh, Miss O'Banion, thank you! Now make a really good wish!" she bubbled.

Eloise abandoned good sense and said without hesitation, "I wish to be working again as an able-bodied educator. Now let's see what you can do, girl."

Waving her wand, Mary Margaret said, "Granted."

Several minutes passed, both women silently watching each other when the phone rang. Eloise got up and walked over to it. Picking it up on the second ring she froze, turned to Mary Margaret and stammered, "I . . . I walked!"

Mary Margaret grinned. "Yes, you did. Now answer your call."

Eloise listened to the male voice over the receiver and finally said, "Yes, sir, oh yes, first thing tomorrow morning!"

Hanging up, she skipped over to Mary Margaret and grasped her hands. "My dear, I'm sorry I gave you such a hard time. My Lord, I can skip! Thank you."

"You have one more wish, you know," Mary Margaret prompted.

"I don't need it!" Eloise said with a laugh. "I've got everything I want. That was Mr. Jordan, Superintendent of Schools. They need me! I start tomorrow."

"I told you, I could do it. Now that other wish," Mary Margaret urged. "The rules are clear cut, I have to grant three wishes."

Eloise stopped hopping with joy and sat back down on the sofa. "I have everything I want. A wish is quite a responsibility, you know."

Sitting, deep in thought, Eloise's old, worn face suddenly creased into a grim grin. "It's time that I practice what I have been preaching all these years." She looked Mary Margaret directly in the eyes. "This will be a real test for you. I wish for an end to world hunger and war."

Mary Margaret grew as white as her crinoline gown. "Miss O'Banion! Surely you don't really want to wish for that."

Eloise eyed the pale young woman coldly, "Too much for you? You always were an underachiever."

"Wishes are supposed to be selfish. That's human nature," Mary Margaret reasoned. "Don't you want to be young? Don't you want a husband, children? How about wealth, security for your old age?"

Laughing, Eloise said, "Youth? God forbid! I've lived my life and I'm satisfied. I couldn't stand another fifty years. As for a husband, it would have been nice . . . but. And I've had over a thousand children to mold and to love. No thank you, my dear. You've already granted me wealth."

Silence filled the room. After a moment, Eloise said, "I wish for an end to world hunger and war."

"But Miss O'Banion, that's impossible!"

Being firm, Eloise used her most teacherly voice. "Not a very effective fairy godmother are you? Maybe I'll just wish for your superiors."

"Come on, Miss O'Banion," Mary Margaret pleaded. "Look it's not that I can't grant your wish, it's just that it would be wrong. You can't go around changing the whole world."

"Why not?" Eloise demanded, taking immense pleasure in tapping her foot.

"Because fighting is a human trait, it's human nature to fight, and hunger is part of living on this earth. You can't change human nature and not alter all of humanity."

Smiling at her ex-student, Eloise exclaimed, "Now that's an astute argument, Mary Margaret! You please me when you use your deductive reasoning. In fact you're the perfect example of your argument, but I can't accept that the world was meant to be such an unhappy place."

Mary Margaret tried one more time. "Miss O'Banion, you're going to put us out of work. People need to have things to wish for!"

"So, you're just being selfish. Well, my wish stands. Grant my wish!" Eloise demanded, her cheeks flushed with anger.

Mary Margaret bowed her head sadly. "I'll talk to my supervisor," she mumbled and vanished. Eloise noticed the gold fairy dust looked duller as it settled on her dark carpet.

Three days later Eloise sat at her kitchen table shaking her head in annoyance while marking papers. A noise distracted her and she looked up. Standing before her was a very morose Mary Margaret.

"Watched the news earlier this evening, there's still a famine in Africa," Eloise said matter-of-factly. "And the world is still trying to blow itself up."

"Miss O'Banion, I've learned something very disturbing." She hesitated then blurted, "Your time's almost up!"

Eloise stared at her fairy godmother in shock. Trying to control the wild pounding of her heart, she asked, "You mean I'm going to die?"

Mary Margaret started crying. Sobbing, she blubbered, "Soon."

"So why are you telling me this?" Eloise asked, already accepting the inevitability of living and dying.

"I thought that you could use your last wish to extend your life. After all, your first wish has caused this. The strain on your heart from all this mobility."

Mary Margaret looked embarrassed as she added, "You see most wishes have a catch, that's why we give you three so you can counteract the negative aspects."

Eloise laughed bitterly, "So that's it, still trying to save your job!"

"No, no!" Mary Margaret gasped. "I'm trying to save you! You've only got a few days."

"Well," Eloise said philosophically. "I've had a good life, longer than all those young boys I taught who went off to war and died. My last days were made happy with your help, so . . ."

"Miss O'Banion, help yourself!" Mary Margaret wailed.

"No, all I can wish for now is to have an end to hunger and war. I'd like to die knowing that I helped mankind."

Mary Margaret asked, "Is that it then?"

"Yes."

"Believe me, Miss O'Banion, you're making a terrible mistake. Please don't make me do this!"

"Mary Margaret, if wishes were fishes, everybody'd eat steak. Well, I want to know that nobody will have to go hungry. I don't care if they eat fish, steak, or broccoli!" Eloise said. Turning back to her papers, she added, "Nice of you to visit."

Weeping uncontrollably, Mary Margaret disappeared with a spray of tear-soaked gray ash instead of gold dust.

A few days later Eloise was marking math papers in front of the television when the broadcast came. A giant asteroid had apparently appeared out of nowhere and was hurtling to the earth at an astonishing speed.

Eloise clutched her hands in prayer and wept. "You really can't change human nature," she cried out, realizing her unyielding sense of righteousness had doomed humanity.

Carrying that burden, all she could do was look up at the darkening sky. Guilt heavy on her conscience and tears wet on her cheeks, Eloise joined the rest of mankind in wishing for a miracle.

PERSONAL
ACKNOWLEDGEMENTS

I'd like to thank everybody who helped me write all the stories in this book including the Writers of the Night (Nancy Bowker, Beverly Haaf and the late Anna Hagman), Elektra Hammond—Until Midnight—for her editing skills, my two children, Kat and Stephen, who inspired many of the stories through their actions while growing up and who helped with their suggestions when I'd write myself into a corner, my sister Roslyn and my friend Marie for being the first to read my stories when they were handwritten, and of course my husband, Tom, who has to stop whatever he's doing to help me whenever my computer acts up and who graciously accepts life with a writer.

JERSEY PINES INK

Look for upcoming books
from Jersey Pines Ink
https://www.jerseypinesink.com/

A new anthology:
Cryptgnats
edited by
Dina Leacock

Death Counts the Golden Coins
Chronicles of JumpRope Book Two
by
Ivy C. Leigh

Diane Arrelle, the pen name of Dina Leacock, has been writing for over 20 years and has sold more than 250 short stories. She has three published books including *Seasons on the Dark Side*, and *Just A Drop In The Cup*.

Diane Arrelle

Growing up extremely rural and listening nightly to the ghastly, ghostly tales that her older siblings forced upon her, Diane naturally turned to horror.

To support her writing habits over the years she has held a wide variety of jobs including Teacher, School Bus Driver, Waitress, Sales Clerk, Mystery Shopper, Holiday Gift Wrapper, Newspaper Columnist, Tutor, Freelance Writer, Senior Citizen Center Director and she was also that person who stood around in a mall burning vanilla flavored milk and cooking tasteless crepes to sell nonstick pots and pans.

She is proud to be one of the founding members and past president of the Garden State Horror Writers as well as a past president of the Philadelphia Writers' Conference. She recently retired from being director of a municipal senior citizen center and is now co-owner of Jersey Pines Ink, a small publishing company.

She lives on the edge of the Pine Barrens (home of the Jersey Devil) in Southern New Jersey with her husband and her cat.

You can visit her at http://www.arrellewrites.com or https://www.jerseypinesink.com